KEEP

FURY BROTHERS
BOOK 2

ANNA HACKETT

Keep

Published by Anna Hackett

Cover by Hang Le Designs

Cover image by Wander Aguiar

Edits by Tanya Saari

ISBN (ebook): 978-1-922414-97-7

ISBN (paperback): 978-1-922414-98-4

ISBN (special edition paperback): 978-1-922414-99-1

WHAT READERS ARE SAYING ABOUT ANNA'S ACTION ROMANCE

Heart of Eon - Romantic Book of the Year (Ruby) winner 2020

Cyborg - PRISM Award Winner 2019

Edge of Eon and Mission: Her Protection - Romantic Book of the Year (Ruby) finalists 2019

Unfathomed and Unmapped - Romantic Book of the Year (Ruby) finalists 2018

Unexplored – Romantic Book of the Year (Ruby) Novella Winner 2017

Return to Dark Earth – One of Library Journal's Best E-Original Books for 2015 and two-time SFR Galaxy Awards winner

At Star's End – One of Library Journal's Best E-Original Romances for 2014

The Phoenix Adventures – SFR Galaxy Award Winner for Most Fun New Series and "Why Isn't This a Movie?" Series

Beneath a Trojan Moon – SFR Galaxy Award Winner and RWAus Ella Award Winner

Hell Squad – SFR Galaxy Award for best Post-Apocalypse for Readers who don't like Post-Apocalypse

"Like Indiana Jones meets Star Wars. A treasure hunt with a steamy romance." – SFF Dragon, review of *Among Galactic Ruins*

"Action, danger, aliens, romance – yup, it's another great book from Anna Hackett!" – Book Gannet Reviews, review of *Hell Squad: Marcus*

Sign up for my VIP mailing list and get your *free box set* containing three action-packed romances.

Visit here to get started: www.annahackett.com

1

MACY

"Mmm." My moan was long and loud.

This was just too good. Heaven on Earth.

I ate the last bite of the delicious, mouthwatering beignet, and moaned again. Of course, that was when my boss decided to walk in.

He'd been away for two days on a job. He was a badass bounty hunter, and he looked it too. He usually took smaller, local jobs, but occasionally, he got called in for big jobs out of state.

Because he was good. Really good.

Colton Fury was also gorgeous.

He was tall, with a muscled bod, and tattoos on his forearms. Add to that combo dark-brown hair and a neat, dark beard, and he sort of oozed grumpy, tough competence. The man was always scowling. Luckily, it worked for him.

Today, he wore dark jeans, and a Henley in navy blue with sleeves that cut into his biceps, and motorcycle boots.

It was really, really lucky that my douchebag of an ex had forced me to swear off men. It meant I was immune to the pull of Colton Fury. Mostly.

He jerked to a halt, his gaze on me. He had blue eyes, and a heavy, intense stare. When Colt gave you his full attention, you felt it.

I was currently sitting cross-legged on top of my desk. I ran his office, did the admin, paid the bills, and manned the phone. Or I should say, womanned the phone. He'd hired me as his admin assistant six months ago, but I'd changed my title to office manager.

If it wasn't for me, everything around here would fall apart.

Colt might track down the bad guys, but I did everything else. And I mean everything. The man was allergic to paperwork.

"Hey." I licked the last of the sugary goodness off my fingers.

His gaze zeroed in on my mouth, and his scowl deepened. "What are you doing?"

"Enjoying the last bit of heavenly goodness that is a beignet from Uptown Coffee. Best beignets in the city. I've made it my mission to try them all, and Café Du Monde is good, but a little overrated."

He grunted.

"I'd offer you one, but I ate them all."

Another grunt. I eyed his flat stomach. I was pretty sure Colt had less than one percent body fat, and didn't eat many beignets. Me, I was lucky to have inherited a killer metabolism from my mother—God rest her soul. I didn't have one-percent body fat, but I could eat what I wanted.

I hopped off the desk and straightened my skirt. Colt constantly bitched about my clothes, not that I cared. Today, I was wearing a flirty gray skirt that was flared to the knee, and I'd paired it with a red halter top. It was summer. I thought it gave a summery professional vibe.

Something flickered in his gaze, and his brow creased. "How did the job go?"

"Fine."

I didn't bother asking if he'd caught the man wanted for several murders. Colt always caught his man.

"What are you wearing?" His voice was a deep, gritty growl.

I slid a hand down my hip. "It's called a skirt, Colt. Professional office wear."

He crossed his brawny arms, and I tried not to let my gaze drift over his tattoos. They were an interesting collection of objects. A house with the word *home* inked under it. A heart with *DF* written inside it. And a few other images, the meaning of which I could only guess at.

"That outfit is *not* professional." He pivoted and stalked into his office.

I followed him. "Hello, what the hell do you know about women's fashion? Or what's professional? You wear jeans and boots to the office every day."

He rocked to a quick stop, and stared at his desk. A desk that was now sparkling clean. I'd dusted it this morning. Thankfully, Colt kept it pretty tidy because of said allergy to paperwork.

"What the fuck is that?" He stabbed a finger at the new object on the corner of his desk.

I tried not to notice his finger, or the rest of his hands. I'd noted before that Colt had amazing hands—large, strong, with long fingers.

"That is a plant. To brighten your office."

His head sliced my way. Oh, his scowl was in fine form. I'd developed a rating system for Mr. Grumpy Bounty Hunter's scowls. Level 1 was his resting scowl. Level 2, he was faintly pissed off at something. Level 3, there was trouble brewing, so watch out. Level 4, he was pissed off and ready to let you know about it. Level 5, batten down the hatches, because he was going to blow.

Tapping my chin, I assessed that his scowl was a 3.5.

"I don't want a plant."

"Sure, you do."

"I don't."

I pouted. "It's a gift, big guy. And it's too late now."

He sighed. "Fine. But I'll kill it."

"That's why I got you a cactus." I turned the little pot around. It was painted in bright colors. "Plus, it matches your spiky temperament. You guys are twinsies."

His blue eyes narrowed.

I smiled. "Looks like you need this as well." I pulled the folded paper out of my pocket.

Colt took the brown origami bear and gave me a bland look. This one was on all fours, looking like it was ready to go in for the kill. Sometimes I just did bear faces—all with varying grumpy looks.

My mom had taught me origami. I loved slipping away from everything for a few precious seconds to create something bright and fun.

I made Colt bears because he was grumpy like a bear. He pulled open his desk drawer, and I caught a glimpse of his growing paper bear collection as he dropped it in.

"I know you just got back, but I have a local job for you. Should be quick." I hitched my hip on the corner of his desk.

"What job?"

"Lenny Bridges skipped bail."

Colt rolled his eyes. "Again?"

I nodded.

"He'll be half drunk on his stool at his favorite bar."

"Yep." Lenny was nothing if not consistent.

"Fine." Colt raked a hand through his hair. "It should only take me an hour."

That's when I heard light, quick steps out in the front office.

A pretty girl of seven burst in. She smiled at me. "Hi, Macy. I *love* your red top."

"Thanks, gorgeous girl."

Then Daisy Fury whirled. "Daddy, you're home!"

A rare smile broke out on Colt's face. As those strong arms wrapped around the little girl, I couldn't look away. I felt weird flutters in my belly.

When he smiled, Colt was devastatingly handsome.

"I missed you, short stuff."

I backed out of the room, waving at Lola—Daisy's nanny, and the Fury brothers' housekeeper. The gray-haired woman cooked and cleaned for all the Fury brothers. Colt had four brothers who between them all owned this entire block of the Warehouse District in New Orleans. They all had their homes and businesses in the area.

I glanced at Colt and Daisy. It was another far too attractive thing about Colton. He was an amazing single father. He adored Daisy, and she adored him back.

Did men know how sexy it was to see them being good dads? I shook my head, then sat back at my desk.

It was really, really lucky I'd sworn off men.

My phone rang and I picked it up. "Colton Fury's office."

Silence.

My hand tightened. "Hello?"

I felt a little shiver of unease. This was the fourth call like this in only two days. I could sense someone on the line.

"When you're ready to talk, I'll be waiting." I set the phone down and shrugged.

Life was too short to worry about things. That was my mom's motto. *Have fun, find adventures, and regret nothing, Macy Moo.*

I did my best to live up to her words every day.

2

COLT

Well, Lenny proved to be as predictable as always.

As I stomped into the dive bar in Mid-City, I spotted a disheveled Lenny Bridges cradling his half-finished beer at the bar. It didn't look like it was his first by the way he was swaying.

I stopped behind him. "Lenny, time to go."

"Fury?" He turned, eyeing me blearily. "Oh, man. Can I finish my beer?"

"No." I pulled him off his stool and looked at the bartender. The grizzled guy looked like he'd seen it all, and it bored him. "He paid?"

The man shook his head. "Nope."

I shook Lenny. "Pay."

Lenny frowned, patting his pockets. "Um, I don't got no money."

With a sigh, I pulled out my wallet and dropped some cash on the bar. Then I hauled Lenny past the pool table toward the door.

"You puke in my truck again, Lenny, and we'll have issues."

My target's answer was a loud burp. A biker babe holding a pool cue stepped in front of us.

"Hi there, big guy."

My scowl deepened. I didn't like her calling me that. Only Macy called me that. I didn't like it when she did it. Mostly.

The woman had big hair, as black as my boots, and a skintight skirt that had left short behind two inches ago. Her red tube top clung to her assets with luck and a prayer.

"Stay." She smiled. "We can play."

Her tone left no doubt that she wasn't talking about pool. As I shot her a look, my mind turned to the red halter top clinging to my petite office assistant, and a mass of blonde hair with gentle curls. And huge, green eyes that were always laughing at me.

"I'm working." I sidestepped the woman, and headed for the door.

"We'd have fun, big guy. The hot and sweaty kind."

I waved a hand without looking back.

"I like fun," Lenny called out.

I heard the woman snort. "No, thanks."

I loaded Lenny into the back of my Suburban. It didn't take long to drop him off at the New Orleans lockup.

Soon, I was headed back to the Warehouse District. To home.

It was nice to be back after several days away, chasing the scum of the Earth. My hands flexed on the wheel. After seeing the worst of what humanity could do, it was nice to get back to my daughter and my brothers. Daisy's smile went a long way to making me feel clean.

I'd sure as hell come a long way from where I'd been born. If I hadn't found my brothers, I could have ended up being the one tracked down by bounty hunters.

I'd been born in a small town in St. Bernard parish. My parents had both been bayou rats, with a liking for white powder. One day, after a rip-roaring argument, my daddy had shot my mom and killed her. He'd gone to jail, and I'd gone into the system.

I'd ended up in some good foster homes, and some shitty ones. Nineteen in total. Eventually, as a sullen teen who'd taken no bullshit, I had ended up in the home of the Tuckers.

The couple had not been nice people. They'd sold the story that they took in wayward boys that no one else wanted to deal with. In reality, Harvey Tucker liked beating boys, while his wife preferred verbal abuse.

You're nothing, boy. Trash.

You're a blight on society. You deserve nothing.

No one cares about you, boy. No one ever will.

My hands flexed on the steering wheel again. One good thing had come of being in the Tuckers' home. I'd met my brothers.

The five of us had bonded, escaping the Tuckers after joining together to stop Harvey Tucker's savage beating of our brother, Reath.

They weren't my brothers by blood, but by choice. We'd run away together, and when we could, we'd changed our surnames to Fury. The one thing that had fueled us. Driven us. It had kept us surviving.

We'd all vowed to make a good life for ourselves.

And we had.

We owned a whole block in the Warehouse District, and we all ran our own successful businesses.

Yeah, we'd come a long way from the shitty childhood we'd escaped.

I parked in front of my office. The brick building had

large windows with just my name, Colton Fury, etched on the glass.

I slid out. My converted warehouse sat behind the office, and connected with the family home my brothers and I had renovated as a central space for all of us. Daisy lived there with Lola, our godsend of a housekeeper. She took care of Daisy when I was away.

Dante and Reath both had adjoining warehouses. Dante's nightclub and restaurants were down the block. Reath ran a security company a few doors down from my office. Beauden ran his gym—Hard Burn—and lived in the apartment above it.

And Kavner had built a slick office tower on the corner to house his billion-dollar businesses. He lived in the penthouse apartment.

I slid my hands into my pockets. Yeah, the Fury brothers had made it.

I pushed open the office door and music hit me. It was something bright and poppy, which made me wince.

My assistant was dancing as she filed things in the filing cabinet. My gaze dropped to her ass. She was a tiny thing, but curvy, and she had a peach of an ass that I'd spent far too much time studying.

The front of my jeans tightened. *Fuck.*

I tried not to think of Macy Underwood's ass, or her slim legs, or her plush lips.

But when she pranced around the office in cute little outfits, it made it really hard. Jesus, I needed to hit a bar and get laid.

She whirled. "You're back? How'd it go with Lenny?"

"Fine."

Her eyebrows rose. "You're in a mood. Or more of a

mood than usual." She folded her arms across her chest, which pushed her breasts up.

Shit. Something in my chest twanged. I didn't like it at all.

My gaze moved to that damn tie around her neck. One simple tug and it would come undone.

It was summer, and Macy was tanned. But there would be parts of her that didn't see the sun, that would be white and smooth. Parts that no one ever saw.

Parts I wanted to see.

"Hello?" She stepped closer and waved a hand in my face. "You in there, big guy?"

Her scent wrapped around me. She always smelled like berries.

Macy wasn't my type. She was too nice, too sunny, too perky. I was...none of those things. I hooked up in bars, and fucked. And that was rarely, since I had a little girl at home, I never brought women back to my place. When was the last time I picked up a woman? I frowned. It had been months.

"I have to go."

Macy frowned. "But you just got here?"

"Got shit to do." I turned and headed out.

Away from the scent of berries, and away from that sweet, little body that was too much temptation.

3

COLT

When I headed into the house, I heard the rumble of deep voices. In the open-plan kitchen and living area, I found my brothers. We tried to eat dinner together a few times a week.

My daughter was perched on Beauden's broad shoulders like a monkey. Lola was bustling around in the kitchen. She loved to cook, and that was lucky for us, as we liked to eat. She was a widow, and her only son lived in London. She loved working for us, and she'd become a member of our family. Best of all, apart from her amazing lasagna, was that she loved Daisy like her own granddaughter.

"Daddy!" Daisy smiled at me, and my chest tightened. There was something about the pure love of the kid. No strings, no conditions.

Becoming a father had never been on my damn radar. It started with my own fucking father. Finding out dear old dad had decided to marry some nutjob woman who'd been writing to him in jail had been a shock.

Discovering she'd had a baby was even worse.

I didn't even want to contemplate how the hell he'd

gotten her pregnant. Unfortunately, I knew you could get just about anything in prison if you had some money.

I blew out a breath. I'd tried hard to connect with my sister. She'd been a wild teenager when we'd first met, coping with having a father in prison for murder, and a less-than-stable mother.

For a long time, I tried, but Chrissy had lost herself to drugs. After the fifth time I'd gotten her into rehab and she'd run away, I'd given up.

I was a bounty hunter. I could've found her, but I didn't...

Then I discovered she'd ODed. My hands clenched on the wheel, my jaw tightened. I should've looked for her.

But the biggest shock of all had been discovering that I had a baby niece who was headed for the foster system. There had been no way in hell I was letting my niece, an innocent girl, get swallowed up by the system.

I'd pulled every string, and called in every favor, and eventually I brought that tiny bundle in a pink blanket home.

Fuck, Daisy had been so tiny. Her big blue eyes were the same shade as mine.

I hadn't known a single thing about babies. I'd been fucking scared I'd drop her.

But she'd needed me. End of story.

Seven years later, she was the light of my damn life.

Daisy's giggle drew me out of my memories. Beau leaned down, and I transferred her onto my shoulders.

"How was your job in Georgia?" Beau looked very much like the former mercenary and fighter he was. He was rugged, tattooed, and as tough as steel. I trusted him with my life. I trusted all of them.

"The ass—" I looked up at Daisy "—prick is going away for a long time."

Reath twisted on a stool at the huge, marble island. "I heard he put up a fight when you cornered him."

Reath was a few years younger than me. Unlike me, who remembered my parents, Reath didn't. He'd been abandoned as a baby. He had a handsome face that we gave him hell for, brown skin, and short, black hair.

I wasn't surprised that he already knew about my Georgia job. He'd spent several years in the CIA, doing shit he never talked about. He'd gone in cocky, and come out lethal, alert, and with parts of him far darker than before.

His company, Phoenix Security Services, did good work, and Reath kept his ear to the ground. He knew all the players in New Orleans, and further afield.

"Yeah, he put up a fight." I smiled darkly. "I was more than happy to teach him a lesson."

Reath nodded, the corner of his lips tipping up.

"Good. From what I heard on the news, the piece of trash deserved it." This came from Kavner, who leaned against the counter, still wearing a suit, but at least he'd shed his jacket and tie. I couldn't believe he was willing to wear ties at all.

"Yeah, the fucker deserves whatever hell he finds in prison."

"Daddy, you owe a dollar for the swear jar."

I scowled. Macy had colluded with Daisy on this fucking swear jar. Just the thought of my assistant had me feeling tense and unsettled.

She was getting under my skin, and I didn't fucking like it.

"There is no swear jar."

"There *is*," Daisy insisted. "Macy's helping me decorate it."

I growled.

"Sorry we're late."

Dante appeared, with his arm around his woman, Mila.

Mila was smiling, her face flushed. Dante looked his usual self—dark hair, dressed in a black button-down shirt, black beard.

My gaze narrowed. He also looked very smug and satisfied. I didn't need three guesses to know why the pair was late.

Mila had been on the run from some bad people. She'd overheard the wrong conversation at work, and it had almost cost her life. She'd ended up getting a job at Dante's nightclub, Ember, in order to hide out. My brother had taken one look at her, and lost his mind.

He'd protected her, gotten her free of her troubles, and fallen in love. Mila was good for him. She made him happy.

"What's for dinner?" Dante asked.

"*Lasagna*," Daisy cried.

Dante tugged on Daisy's hair. "My favorite."

"Mine too," my daughter said.

We were eating early, because Dante and Mila worked nights at the club. Mila worked on PR and marketing for the club, as well as Dante's neighboring bar, Smokehouse, and his two restaurants.

"Everyone, sit at the table," Lola ordered.

Everyone moved. I set Daisy down, then headed for the fridge, and nabbed a beer.

"You okay?"

I looked up at Beau. "The job's done. I'm home."

"You seem...unsettled."

I shrugged a shoulder. "I'm good."

Beau's gaze lingered, but he nodded. "If you need to blow off some steam, come to the gym." A faint smile crossed his rugged face. "I'll beat you up for a bit."

I snorted. "I can hold my own, old man." Beau was the oldest, but only by a few years. We still liked to give him hell about it.

"I'll show you, old man," he grumbled.

"Sit, you two." Lola pushed between us, waving a hand. "Time to eat."

I sat down, my little girl chattering in my ear, surrounded by my brothers.

No bad guys, and no tempting assistant.

This was just what I needed.

4

MACY

Taming my mass of hair was never easy. I had some curls, not tight ones, but just enough to make things challenging.

I decided to leave it loose today, even though I knew the humidity would wreak havoc on it.

Music played—Taylor's latest hit, of course—and I danced my way into the kitchen. There was plenty to be happy about. The sky was blue, the sun was shining, it was summer. Even the humidity couldn't dampen my mood.

Sometimes I missed San Francisco. Those sweeping views of the Bay and the majesty of the Golden Gate Bridge, but New Orleans more than made up for it. I loved the vibe of the city—sexy, a little mysterious, a little quirky.

Mostly what I missed about San Francisco were the memories of my mother. Losing her to cancer had been the worst thing in my life. Since I was little, it'd just been the two of us. The man who'd fathered me had taken off before I was even born.

Just the two of us, Macy Moo. We can take on the world. Keep rolling, have adventures. Live free.

My mother had always had more than a little hippie in her.

I popped a bagel in the toaster and pulled the cream cheese out of the fridge. The scent of coffee filled the kitchen thanks to the timer on my coffee machine.

I cha-cha-ed across the kitchen, once again so grateful that I'd found this place. It was a cute little shotgun house in Freret, painted a bright blue, with a red door. The best thing, it was close enough that I could ride my bicycle to work.

Thinking about the things I needed to do today, I started a mental list. I needed Colt to sign some paperwork. I wrinkled my nose. I'd probably need to tie the man down.

Ooh. A naughty image of Colt—shirtless and tied to a bed—popped into my head.

I took a second to appreciate it, then squashed it.

No fantasizing about your boss, Macy.

In desperate need of coffee, I reached for my favorite mug. It was rainbow colored, with words on the side that said *First Coffee, then the Adventures*. It had been a gift from my mom. When I found the spot where I kept it empty, I frowned.

Weird. Wrinkling my nose, I scanned the countertop. I always kept it right there by the coffee machine. It was a superstitious little ritual of mine.

It wasn't in the sink either. *What the hell?* I lived alone. No one could've moved it.

Turning, I spotted it on the table. With the handle broken off.

A chill ran down my spine.

Had I put it there and forgotten? I didn't remember breaking it. Had I sleepwalked?

The toaster dinged and my bagel popped up.

Fighting off my disquiet, I spread cream cheese on the bagel, and found another mug. I hated this feeling. Nervous and unsettled, second-guessing myself. I hadn't felt it too much since I'd left California and settled in New Orleans.

Shaking my head, I took a bite of bagel and poured my coffee into the other mug. I added lots of vanilla syrup and creamer.

I needed to get moving. I'd solve my mug mystery later.

Heading outside, I looked up and then unlocked my bike from the side of the house. I smiled. It was something else that gave me pure joy. The bike was bright turquoise, with a woven basket on the front.

I swung my leg over the seat. Today I was wearing capri pants in dark blue, and a bright-yellow-and-white shirt. Setting off down the street, I lifted my face to the sunshine. I spotted Mrs. Lawrence at the end of the street, watering her flowers.

"Hi, Mrs. L."

The old lady smiled and waved.

I decided I needed to butter Colt up for the paperwork —or rather, sugar him up. The man had a secret weakness for the blueberry muffins from Uptown Coffee. I turned left. I'd make a quick stop there first.

The traffic thickened. Gripping my handlebars, I focused on staying where I needed to be. When I reached the coffee shop, I chained my bike up and headed inside.

The place has a warm wood floor, dotted with tables, and a long counter. The counter was dominated by a huge coffee machine, and a glass cabinet filled with baked goods.

"Morning, Macy." The young, goth woman working behind the counter nodded at me. She wore a shirt with a skull-and-flower design on it, and had a white apron tied around her waist.

"Hi, Raven. Cool shirt. Can I get six blueberry muffins, please?"

"I'll get them." Dean appeared. He was another regular worker at the coffee shop.

I smiled at him. "Thanks, Dean."

The young man smiled back. He was a few years younger than me, quiet, but always nice.

"Are these for you?" he asked.

"No. A bribe for my boss. Super-grump extraordinaire."

"Sounds bad," Raven said.

"Oh, no. He's mostly all bark, and he's a great dad. You should see him with his little girl."

"So he's married?" Dean asked casually, holding out the bag to me.

"Nope. Single dad." I handed over the cash and took the bag. "I'd better get going. Have a great day."

Outside, I set the bag of muffins in the basket of my bike and set off.

I hadn't gone far down the street when I heard the roar of an engine. I glanced back over my shoulder and my pulse spiked. A big, dark truck was gunning down the street. He was going too fast, and he was too close to the edge of the road.

The asshole was going to crowd me.

I gripped the handlebars and edged over as far as I could.

"Move over, asshole," I muttered.

He roared past and knocked me.

The world spun. I went flying, and hit the pavement between two parked cars.

I felt a sting on my elbows, and the air was knocked out of me. My butt throbbed, having taken the brunt of my impact.

My bike! I could see the front tire was bent.

Dismay, fear, and anger churned inside me. I just sat there, stunned.

"Macy!"

Dean and Raven raced out of the coffee shop.

"Are you all right?" Dean said.

"My bike... There was a truck..."

"I saw the dick. He was going too fast." Dean helped me onto the sidewalk, and Raven rescued my damaged bike.

I felt shaky now.

Dean shook his head. "You could've been seriously hurt."

"Is there someone we should call?" Raven asked.

My hand shook as I pulled my phone out of my pocket. "I'll call him." I blew out a breath.

I was all right. I wasn't hurt. Everything was fine.

I swiped the screen and called Colt.

5

COLT

Finishing a phone call, I leaned back in my office chair. I'd had an old, battered, brown leather one for years, that always creaked like hell. Two months back, while I was away on a job, Macy had donated the damn thing and gotten me a new, black, ergonomic one.

I'd yelled. She'd rolled her eyes.

"Your back will thank me, big guy."

Later that day, I'd found one of her bloody origami bears —with claws raised and a scowl drawn on it—in the center of my desk.

This new chair was the most comfortable thing I've ever sat in. Not that I'd ever tell her that.

I wondered where the hell she was. She wasn't usually late. She had the annoying habit of being constantly early.

No doubt she'd skip in shortly, after riding that ridiculous green bike of hers, wearing some outfit that made it impossible not to look at her and wonder...things.

Muttering under my breath, I grabbed my coffee mug and sipped. I grimaced. The coffee had gone cold.

I wondered if Macy would leave her hair loose, or wear

it up in a ponytail today. When it was loose, the curls were everywhere. It made me imagine it spread out on a set of bedsheets. My hands sinking into it, clenching on it. She had freckles across her shoulders. And a little mole on the side of her neck. Occasionally, I wondered where else she had them.

I shook my head. Macy was my office assistant. I wasn't supposed to be fantasizing about her.

My phone rang and I snatched it up with more enthusiasm than normal. "Fury."

"Colt?"

I straightened. Macy sounded wrong, shaky. "Macy, where are you?"

A harsh breath rattled across the line. "I got knocked off my bike by this truck—"

I jerked my feet, my hand clenching on the phone. "Are you hurt?"

"Not really."

My stomach felt like rocks at the idea of her being hit by a fucking truck.

"I mean, my elbows are bleeding, but—"

"You're *bleeding*?" My voice sounded like grit. I snatched my keys off my desk. "Do not move." She could have a head injury, or internal bleeding. "I'm on the way. Where are you?"

"The Uptown Coffee on—"

"I know where it is. Do not move."

My chest was tight, my gut was tight, everything was tight as I stalked out to my Suburban.

Seconds later, I was speeding down the street, my hands clenched on the wheel. I'd told her not to ride that damn bike. If she'd fallen the other way, under the vehicle...

A wave of dizziness hit me.

Finally, I saw Uptown Coffee ahead, and spotted a parking space on the street. I pulled in, slamming on the brakes. When my boots hit the pavement, I saw her sitting on the ground. A young man with ridiculous floppy hair, and a woman who clearly thought black was the only color on the color wheel, were hovering over her.

My gaze narrowed. The guy was really close, holding Macy's hand.

I crouched in front of her. "Macy."

"Colt." Relief filled her face.

That's when I saw the graze on her jaw. "I told you not to ride that damn bike."

Tears welled in her eyes, but I saw something else. That spark that was all Macy.

"Some *asshole* in a huge truck hit me. It wasn't my fault! He was speeding, and he was all the way over—" Her voice broke.

I pulled her hand free of floppy hair's hand. The young guy glared at me.

Her palms were grazed as well. *Shit*. I hated seeing her golden skin marred.

"Did you hit your head?"

She swiped at the tears. "No. And I had my helmet on. It's mostly just shock." She lifted her arm and I saw her bleeding elbow. "And some scrapes."

I couldn't handle her blood or her tears. I yanked her into my arms.

"You're okay," I growled.

She snuggled into me, and blew out a shaky breath. "Yeah. I am now."

Damn, she felt so tiny. The idea of the danger she'd been in made me scowl.

I rose, lifting her with me.

"My bike..."

I hadn't even noticed it. I saw the front wheel was twisted and my scowl deepened. I'd find whoever the asshole was who'd hit her, and make him pay.

"You have your scary face on."

She didn't seem all that scared. "I'm going to find who did this."

She slid her arm along my shoulders. I felt the touch through my Henley.

"It was an accident, Colt."

"So, you're her boss?" the young guy said.

"Oh, Dean and Raven, thanks for helping me. These guys are from the coffee shop."

I pretended to ignore the girl in black mouthing *hot* to Macy. A hundred dollars Raven wasn't the name on her birth certificate. Dean glared at me some more.

After I'd gotten Macy settled in my SUV, I went back and grabbed her bike.

"Don't forget the muffins in the basket," she called out.

"You're worried about muffins?" I gritted out.

"Sugary baked goods are always a serious business." She smiled, and I was just damn happy to see some color back in her cheeks. "And I got them for you. Blueberry."

For me? I loved blueberry muffins. I looked at the bag and shook my head. Then I shoved her bike in the back of my SUV.

"No more bike riding." I got in and slammed the driver's side door behind me.

"But Colt—"

"I'll pick you up from now on."

6

MACY

"Ow."

I tried to yank my hand away, but Colt held on tight.

"Got to clean this." He wiped an antiseptic-soaked cloth over my scraped palm.

It's stung like crazy. "It's worse than falling off my bike."

He'd already cleaned my elbows. That had been fun. Not.

"You didn't fall." A muscle ticked in his jaw.

"Hey." I grabbed his wrist. "I'm okay."

He grumbled under his breath, then tossed the bloody cloth down, and got another from the giant first aid kit he kept in the office.

"Jaw."

I pressed a hand to my cheek. "Oh, no. It's fine."

A Level 2 scowl formed. "Germs."

I sighed and lifted my chin. "Fine, but if I cry, it's your fault."

He froze. "There will be no crying."

"You can't control crying, Colt."

"Yes, you can."

"It's a natural reaction." I figured badass bounty hunters could control whether they cried or not, but I couldn't. I cried at TV commercials with cute kids, and anytime I saw pictures of animals stuck in cages at shelters.

"You can control it when the circumstances require it."

I studied Colt's face, and sensed something else. A darker undertone to his words.

My heart squeezed. I knew he'd grown up in foster care, but I didn't know the details. It wasn't something he talked about. Honestly, it was hard to imagine Colt as a kid. I was pretty sure he'd been born as a badass bounty hunter, complete with scowl.

He leaned in, his face just an inch from mine as he cleaned the graze on my jaw.

My heart did an extra thump. He smelled like limes and man. I couldn't exactly describe what man smelled like, but every woman knew it was a scent that made you think of strong arms around you, and lips pressed to the back of your neck.

I shifted my gaze and it collided with his ice-blue eyes. We both went still. Suddenly, I was aware of the fabric of my shirt against my skin. He breathed in, and something flickered in his gaze.

"Macy—"

"Oh, my gosh, Macy, are you hurt?" Daisy bounced into the office, and we jerked apart. Lola followed, eyeing us. A smile flickered on her face.

Colt cleared his throat. "Hi, short stuff."

Daisy put a hand on her dad's arm. "What happened to Macy?"

"I fell off my bike. I'm fine. Your dad's patching me up." I gave the girl a smile.

Daisy's brows drew together. "You're sure you're okay?"

"Positive."

"All done." Colt snapped the first aid kit closed.

"Now you have to kiss it," Daisy said.

My eyes widened. "Huh?"

"When daddy fixes my boo-boos, he always kisses them better." She gestured, watching expectantly.

Colt's brow creased. "Dai, that's for kids' boo-boos."

I could see Lola hiding a smile.

"No." Daisy got a stubborn look that was near-identical to Colt's. "It always makes it feel better, Daddy. You want Macy to feel better, don't you?"

I heard him draw in a deep breath. "Yeah."

His gaze caught mine, and he leaned in. I stayed still—hell, I couldn't have moved if I'd wanted to.

His citrusy smell hit me, and I felt the brush of his beard, then his lips touching my jaw.

My belly clenched, and I felt a pulse between my legs. Oh. *God.*

Then he jerked back and shot to his feet.

"I have to...go," he said.

I blinked. "Okay."

"Daddy, you're dropping Lola and me at the Children's Museum. Then we're going to get the streetcar back."

"Right. And then I'm...meeting a contact."

Clearing my throat, I stood up. "And I need to get some work done." I paused. "Thanks, Colt."

He nodded, then before I knew it, I had the office to myself.

I scrubbed my hands over my face. Right, time to restart the day on the right note. Maybe I'd steal one of Colt's blueberry muffins. He'd carried the bag in when we'd arrived.

But when I scanned his desk, that's when I realized the bag was gone.

I smiled. He'd taken them with him.

Instead, I made myself some iced tea in the tiny kitchen, then got started on emails.

Colt's office had been a disaster when I'd first arrived. With Colt allergic to office work, and out a lot, and a string of assistants he'd frightened off in quick succession, the filing had been a mess, and nothing had been computerized.

I'd fixed that. I'd had a few office-manager jobs in the past. I was good at organizing things, and I liked chatting with people.

The front door opened, and I turned. My smile flattened a little.

It was an older man, bald, with the stocky body of a man who'd once been fit, but had let himself go a little. His rusty-red shirt strained over a barrel-like gut.

"Can I help you?" I managed a polite smile.

He sneered. "I'm here to give you a warning."

"I'm sorry?" There was a panic button under my desk, and it went straight to Reath Fury's security firm down the street. I edged closer to my desk.

"Name's Rawson. Frank Rawson."

The name meant nothing to me. "And?"

"I'm a new bounty hunter in town. Let your boss know not to step on my territory."

Really? I crossed my arms. "Look, Mr. Rawson, you can talk to Colton, but I suspect you waited until he'd left before you came in here to bluster and bully. Colt takes whatever jobs he wants. And he's good." I tipped my nose up. "I'm certain the jobs he takes are ones you can't do."

Anger crossed the man's face, and my pulse skittered. Okay, maybe baiting the jackass was not my greatest idea.

He took a few steps forward. I refused to step back and show any fear.

"I think I should teach you a lesson, little girl."

"I'm not a girl, I'm an adult woman. You can call me Ms. Underwood. Now look, I've had a trying morning. So if you could just leave—"

He took another menacing step forward. "No one tells me what to do, you uppity bitch."

Neither of us heard the door open.

"Who the fuck are you?"

Colt's lethal voice made my head jerk up.

He stood in the doorway, looking like some dark, avenging angel. No, not an angel. There was nothing angelic about Colton Fury. Demon hunter. He was a dark, avenging demon hunter.

Hmm, maybe I'd been reading too much paranormal romance lately.

"Colt, Mr. Rawson is a new bounty hunter in town. He came to introduce himself." My tone was flat and unimpressed.

Frank Rawson turned, and I saw him eye Colt, then swallow.

Yep, Rawson was one of those bullies who liked to push around people he thought were weaker than him.

"Rawson, you want to explain why you're in my office assistant's face?"

"Office manager," I interjected.

Colt ignored me. "And why you're calling her names?"

"Fury, I just—" Rawson put on a jovial, old boy tone.

Colt was not having it. He strode to Rawson and gripped the front of the man's shirt, then towed him to the door. "Outside. Now."

They disappeared, and I let my shoulders sag. What a

day. It seemed I was attracting assholes left, right, and center.

My phone rang.

I lifted it to my ear. "Colton Fury's office."

Silence.

I frowned. "Are you there?"

Nothing, but I sensed somebody.

"Look, I don't have time for this right now. I've reached my asshole quota for the day." I slammed the phone down.

Colt returned a minute later, alone. "You don't have to worry about Rawson."

Before I could respond, Colt disappeared into his office, and closed the door.

I dropped into my chair. I really wished I had one of those blueberry muffins, right about now.

7

COLT

Grunting, I slammed my fist into the punching bag. My shirt was soaked with sweat.

Thud. Thud. Thud.

I kept hitting the bag, trying to burn off some energy. Trying to burn off the low hum of desire.

Fuck. There was no way I was lusting after my office assistant. She was off limits. Macy worked for me, and she wasn't my type. I didn't do cute, or sweet, or perky.

I landed another heavy punch. The familiar sounds of Hard Burn echoed around me. The slaps of fists against punching bags, treadmills whirring, the grunts of guys sparring in the boxing rings.

My brothers and I all worked out at Beau's gym. It had turned into *the* place to train in New Orleans. A lot of guys wanted to train with Beauden Fury.

Thud. Thud. Thud.

My brain served me up some images of Macy after she'd been knocked off her bike. Grazed and shaken. My gut churned. The thought of her hurt was unacceptable.

The next image was Macy on her desk, looking at me with lips swollen from my kiss.

My jaw tightened. *Dammit.*

"Hmm, looks like a man with a problem."

Kav's amused voice made me stiffen.

"Woman trouble," Beau said. "Only woman trouble would send him here in the middle of the day to destroy one of my punching bags."

"Don't you two have better things to do." I glanced at them over my shoulder.

Beau crossed his brawny arms. "This is my gym. Checking in with my customers is my job."

Kav waved a hand at his workout gear. "I'm doing a lunchtime workout."

Most people only saw Kav's money and designer suits, but I knew that he kept in shape.

"I'm working out too."

My brothers studied me like I was a damn lab rat, and I fought not to glare at them. They knew me better than anyone.

"Looks to me like you're working out your frustration." Kav's lips tipped into a smile. "Unsuccessfully."

I growled. I pulled my boxing gloves off, then started undoing my wraps.

"Avoiding the issue." Kav looked at Beau.

Beau nodded. "Yep."

"If you've got something to say, say it," I said.

"You're wound up very tight over your pretty office manager," Kav said.

"Assistant," I bit out.

The assholes grinned at each other.

"And I'm not. She's just my employee." I turned, shoving my gear into my bag.

"Oh?" Kav's tone was breezy. "So you wouldn't mind if I asked her out?"

I whirled, my hands turning to fists at my side.

Kav grinned at me.

Fucker. I fought to unclench my teeth. "She's off-limits."

"I like her," Beau said. "She's good for you. Loosens you up a bit."

"I don't do relationships. I have a daughter."

"That doesn't mean you can't be in a relationship, Colt," Kav said.

"I'm not built for them. Daisy gets all my focus."

Kav shook his head. "Just because you haven't tried being in a relationship, doesn't mean it isn't for you."

"Look at Dante," Beau said. "He and Mila are working out great."

I shouldered my gym bag. "I don't want to discuss this."

"No, you're just going to keep beating up innocent punching bags," Kav said. "And watching Macy when you think she isn't looking. You really think what you feel will just disappear?"

If I ignored it long enough, it would. "Yeah."

Kav rolled his eyes to the ceiling.

"You aren't the poster child for committed relationships, Mr. Playboy."

My brother shrugged. "I like women. But I don't make promises I can't keep, and I don't cheat."

"You don't keep the same woman around long enough to cheat," Beau said.

"Whose side are you on?"

"Look guys, drop it—" My cell phone beeped. I pulled it out and saw a text from Lola. "I've got to go. Lola has to run some errands, so I need to get Daisy."

"Colton, ask your sassy office manager, sorry, I mean assistant, out for dinner," Kav said.

"No." I shouldered past them.

"How long until sexual frustration drives him crazy?" Kav asked Beau.

"I give him a week."

"Too optimistic." I could feel Kav's gaze on my shoulder blades. "Three days."

I shot them the finger, then headed out of the gym.

I was keeping my hands—and everything else—off Macy Underwood.

8

MACY

I was playing some music and singing—and okay, dancing—as I did some work in the office.

Whenever Colt was out, I liked to play some tunes. This afternoon, I really needed some upbeat music. My elbows were stinging like crazy and if I stopped, I could still hear the roar of that truck as it got closer to me.

Stop thinking about it, Macy. You're fine.

I threw myself into belting out the chorus of the song when the music cut off. I spun to find Colton and Daisy standing there, both wearing identical scowls.

I bit the inside of my mouth to stop from smiling. It was funny to see Colt's level 3 scowl on his daughter's cute face.

"Hey, you two. How was the museum this morning, Daisy?"

"Good." She scratched her arm. "How are your boo boos?"

"I'm doing all right."

"I need to head out," Colt said. "I'm meeting some informants."

I knew he cultivated strong relationships with a

network of informants. It was something that helped him be so successful at his job.

"I can come too," Daisy said in a huffy tone.

Uh-oh. I looked at Colt.

"Lola's running some errands."

"Ahh."

"I can be nice," Daisy insisted. "I can help you."

Colt crossed his arms. "There are some people out there who are not nice."

Daisy crossed her arms too. Another Colt move that had me coughing to hide the urge to laugh.

"You shouldn't be friends with mean people, Daddy."

"I'm going to places a little girl shouldn't go."

Her pointed chin went up. "I'm *not* little."

Okay, I decided to help him out. "I'd love some company." I opened my desk drawer and pulled out a multi-colored stack of my origami paper. "I can teach you to make some origami. For your dad."

I saw the spark of interest in her blue eyes. She wavered.

I started folding one sheet. "Your dad likes bears."

"No, I don't."

"I want to make a bear for daddy." Daisy crossed to my desk. Behind her, Colt rolled his eyes to the ceiling.

"We'll be fine." I made a shooing motion with my hand.

He nodded, then stepped toward the door. He paused. "Thanks."

That word sounded a little rusty. I watched him stalk out the door. "All right, gorgeous girl, let's get to work." I kicked off my shoes, sat down on the floor, and started folding. Daisy dropped down beside me with a sheet of bright purple paper in her hand.

"Can you teach me to make a bear?"

"I sure can."

Daisy's grumpy mood evaporated quickly. Especially after we left a small army of colored bears in various poses on Colt's desk. I grinned as I imagined his face when he saw them.

"Who taught you to make origami, Macy?"

"My mom."

"Oh." Daisy looked at the floor. "My mom died when I was a baby."

"I know, sweetheart." Sympathy filled me. "I'm sorry."

"Daddy isn't my real daddy. He's actually my uncle, but became my daddy."

"He loves you. I know it hurts not to have your mom, but you're lucky to have your daddy. And your uncles and Lola."

Daisy nodded, fiddling with some of the paper. "Do you have uncles? And a daddy?"

I shook my head. "It was just me and my mom. Now it's just me."

A worried look crossed the little girl's face, and she grabbed my hand. "You have us now. You can have my dad. And my uncles."

A laugh escaped me. There was a fantasy that any red-blooded woman would love—the Fury brothers all to herself. I cleared my throat. "Thanks, Daisy. You don't need to worry about me. I'm happy. I'm free to travel, and have lots of adventures. My mom believed you should have fun and be happy. That life should be filled with new experiences."

Daisy frowned. "I like adventures."

"Good."

"But I like home too."

My belly tightened.

"I like when my uncles come for dinner. And when my daddy hugs me. And when Lola makes lasagna." Daisy's gaze met mine. "I love my bedroom, and when my daddy tucks me in at night and reads me a story."

My heart squeezed. "That sounds pretty wonderful." My mom hadn't tucked me in. She'd just let me go to bed whenever I'd felt like it. I cleared my thick throat. "Okay. What do you want to learn to make next?"

Daisy smiled. "A bird!"

I ran through my entire repertoire of origami—except for the naughty ones I knew—by the time Colt returned. Lola was with him.

Daisy proudly showed Colt his bear-covered desk. I saw a muscle tick beside his eye, but his lips twitched. The little girl gave me a huge hug before she skipped off with Lola.

"Thanks for watching her," Colt said gruffly.

"It's a pleasure. She's a good girl." I picked up some balled-up paper from some of Daisy's errors. I tossed them in the recycling box, and when I spun, I found Colt close behind me. Startled, I lost my balance and stumbled back.

I fell on my butt, and whacked my grazed elbow against the side of my desk.

"*Ouch.*" I cradled my arm to my chest.

"Macy." He scooped me up like I weighed nothing.

My belly fluttered. "I'm okay. Just a klutzy moment."

He set me down on my desk, and gently held my arm up, studying my elbow. "It's bleeding again." He sounded mad.

"My butt feels worse. It took the brunt of my fall today."

His gaze dropped to my lower body, and a funny look crossed his face. "Don't move." He headed for the kitchen, coming back with the first aid kit again.

"I'm going to have to order some stuff to restock that," I said.

Colt removed the bloody bandage from my elbow, face focused as he cleaned my graze. He leaned in close, and I breathed him in. That lime scent of his made me want a gin and tonic.

"There." He pressed a fresh bandage against my graze.

"Thanks."

He lifted his head and our gazes met. My chest felt tight, like a rubber band was pulling taut inside me. I watched as he lowered his head toward my elbow, and his lips brushed the bandage.

"Can't have Daisy finding out I didn't kiss your boo-boo."

"That's not where I want you to kiss me." I froze. Oh God, had that really slipped out?

His blue gaze locked on mine, and I could barely breathe. His eyes were hot and turbulent.

I wasn't sure who moved first. Colt stepped closer, and I widened my legs to make room for him.

Then his mouth was on mine.

He gripped the back of my neck, holding me tight as his mouth took mine. It wasn't a gentle kiss. No, Colton Fury kissed exactly how I imagined he would—rough, bossy, hot.

His tongue stroked mine, and I gripped his arms and moaned. I was acutely aware of him: his touch, his taste, his bulk, his scent, and the scrape of his beard on my skin.

He hauled me closer, kissing me like he owned my mouth. Like he'd starve without his mouth on mine.

I clung to him, a hot achiness building inside me. My head dropped back, and his teeth raked down my neck. "Colt—"

And just like that, I ruined it.

He froze, then yanked his mouth off my skin. He stepped back, a scowl morphing on his rugged face. "*Fuck*."

I swallowed. Not exactly what I was hoping for. "Colt..."

"That shouldn't have happened." He took another step back, like I had an infectious disease.

He shoved a hand through his hair. Then he gave me one long, unreadable look, then spun and stomped into his office.

I pressed my hands to my hot cheeks. A bunch of conflicting emotions zoomed around inside me. Want, need, and desire, mixed with some other things I wasn't quite ready to untangle.

Colt was officially the most gorgeous, confusing man I'd ever met.

"Hello?"

I jolted and turned my head. A young deliveryman stood at the front door.

"Oh, hi." I slid off the desk and smoothed out my clothes. I hope I didn't look like I'd just been kissed senseless by my boss.

"Delivery for Macy Underwood."

"That's me." I signed for it, and took the box from him. "Thanks."

The man left with a salute.

I set the box on my desk and grabbed some scissors. After slicing the tape, I flipped the top of the box open. Then I frowned. There was another box inside. I opened that, and found another smaller box.

With an exasperated huff, opened that one. Then I stilled and my frown deepened. It was empty.

Okay, this was weird. I checked the label. It just had my

name and the address of the office on it. There was no sender listed.

Someone was messing with me.

A strange sensation curled through me. The same one I got when I answered the phone and no one spoke.

I set my shoulders back. I'd already dealt with being knocked off my bike and kissed by Colt. An empty box didn't even make it onto my list of worries.

Shaking my head, I broke down the boxes for recycling. Then I glanced at Colt's closed door and sighed. I was ready for this day to be over. I just wanted to head home and forget my problems. I decided I deserved take out, a glass of wine, and a bubble bath.

No crazy drivers, no weird deliveries, and no hot bosses who gave you the best kiss ever then told you that it shouldn't have happened.

9

COLT

Something was off with Macy.

Maybe the fall off her bike, and then that asshole Rawson, had rattled her.

Or maybe it was because I was a weak asshole and I'd kissed her.

There was no way I'd ever tell her, or anyone, that I'd jacked off last night thinking about that kiss. A fucking kiss had made me shoot all over my own damn gut.

Stop thinking about the kiss. My mouth flattened as I wrestled for some control.

She'd given me her usual smile when I picked her up today, but a few times I'd found her staring off into space at her desk, a worried look on her face.

Macy didn't do worried. I'd never met anyone as relentlessly and annoyingly optimistic in my life.

One other thing was wrong. She hadn't left me any origami today.

"Macy?"

She jolted. "Colt? Do you need something?"

"Are you all right?"

She straightened. "I'm fine."

"How are your elbows and hands?"

She held her hands up. "They're just grazes. I'm made from tough stuff."

I'd tried to find the truck that had hit her, but there hadn't been any CCTV in front of the coffee shop. I scowled. The fucker deserved a talking-to.

There was a knock at the front door. "Special delivery."

My brother Reath stepped inside, holding Daisy's hand.

"Hi, Daddy. Hi, Macy." She skipped in and hugged me. "Macy, are your boo-boos all right today?"

"They sure are, sweetheart."

It was the first real smile I'd seen on her. I felt a tug in my chest, and found myself a little envious that my daughter was on the receiving end of it.

"Thanks for watching Daisy this morning," I said to Reath.

"Always a pleasure." Reath winked at Daisy. "I am her favorite uncle, after all."

Daisy blew him a kiss.

"And the kid is a whiz on the computer."

"I'm going to be a hacker when I grow up," Daisy announced.

I stiffened. "What?"

"With a cool code name and everything. I'm gonna work for Uncle Reath."

Macy giggled, and I scowled at her. She elbowed me and lowered her voice. "She wanted to be a ballerina last week. Don't get too worried, Daddy."

I got a whiff of berries, and barely resisted the urge to sniff her hair.

"Hey, Daisy. Look." Macy drew a piece of colored paper out of her desk drawer. Her fingers moved methodically as she folded. She had small, delicate fingers.

In my head, I imagined them all over my skin—pretty gold against my darker tone.

Fuck.

The last thing I needed was a hard-on with my daughter and brother in the room. Especially my ex-CIA brother, who rarely missed a thing.

Sure enough, Reath was eyeing me with a speculative gaze. He looked at Macy, then back at me, and grinned.

Scowling, I barely resisted giving him the finger. Reath loved to push buttons.

"Oh, I love it," Daisy cried.

Macy handed over the blue butterfly, and Daisy held it like it was made of gold. As my daughter threw her arms around Macy's hips, my assistant hugged my kid.

My chest did that thing with the tug again.

On the plus side, though, at least Macy was looking more like her usual self.

"Daddy, you promised me ice cream."

I stroked my chin. "You sure? I don't recall that."

"Daddy!" Daisy slapped her hands against my gut. "You did. You said at breakfast."

"Hmm, I'm trying to remember..."

"Dad-dy!"

I tickled her, loving her giggles. Not one day went by that I regretted my decision to raise her. I hadn't been sure I was the best man to be a father, but with my brothers' help, and the godsend that was Lola, I was doing a decent job.

"Ice cream, it is."

"Yay." Daisy bounced.

I looked over her head. "Macy, you're coming, too."

She cocked a brow. "Was that an invitation?"

"No. You're coming." I wasn't leaving her in the office alone. And I knew she loved ice cream.

"Please, Macy?" Daisy pleaded.

My assistant rolled her eyes. "It's lucky I can't resist ice cream."

"Yay," Daisy said.

"Reath?" I looked at my brother.

He had a shit-eating grin on his face. "Sorry. I can't. You three have a good time."

When Daisy and Macy headed for the door, I shot him the finger behind their backs. His grin just widened.

Not long after, I was seated at Ice Cream 504—which made the best ice cream in New Orleans, according to Daisy—realizing that I was in my own personal hell.

Daisy was chattering and eating her disgusting looking bubblegum ice cream that was an eye-searing, unnatural shade of blue-green. But my gaze was mostly on Macy as she licked her strawberry cheesecake ice cream.

I shifted on my chair and swallowed a curse. My jeans were getting tight with every glimpse of her pink tongue. She wasn't licking daintily. No, it was all giant, enthusiastic licks of that little tongue, interspersed with moans.

"Colt?"

My gaze flicked up to hers.

"Your ice cream is melting."

I grunted, then took a bite of my own ice cream.

Macy smiled. "I knew you'd get plain chocolate."

"Because it's the best."

"Hi there, welcome to Ice Cream 504." A young guy in an apron appeared. His gaze was locked on Macy.

He held up a tray. "Would you like to try a sample of our new flavor? It's Donut."

"Yes," Daisy cried loudly.

"Dai, lower the volume a notch, yeah?"

My girl nodded, then took a little sample cup.

The man ignored me, smiling at Macy.

She smiled back and took one as well. "Thanks."

Daisy slurped up her sample. "Oh, it's good, Macy."

Ice cream boy perked up. "Oh, you aren't her mom? I mean, you don't look old enough."

"Thanks." I glared at him. "You can go now."

Macy juggled her cone and tried the sample. She gave another little moan. "Oh, that is good."

The guy beamed, then shot a nervous look at me, then resolutely looked back at Macy. "So, are you single—?"

"Go away now." I intensified my glare. I could tell the guy thought about arguing, but he eventually moved on.

"That sounds like grump level 5," Macy said.

I grunted.

She licked her damn ice cream again, and my cock throbbed hard. I noticed a smear of ice cream at the corner of her mouth.

Without thinking, I reached out to wipe it off, just as she licked. Her tongue laved my thumb. She froze, and my blood turned to lava.

Big, green eyes locked on my face. Then, deliberately, she licked my thumb again.

I shuddered. Desire was like fire in my gut. Her eyes widened, and I pulled my hand back, then licked my thumb right where her tongue had touched.

Heat filled her cheeks, and her lips parted.

She was thinking about sex. About me touching her.

"Daddy, your ice cream is dripping."

Daisy's voice snapped me back to reality. My damn cone wasn't the only thing that was dripping.

Mentally cursing, I focused on my damn ice cream. I needed to get some control on this situation.

10

MACY

When I walked back into the office, I was grateful for the air conditioning.

I felt hot and fluttery. I pressed a hand to my belly, glad that Colt had taken Daisy back home. It gave me a few minutes to get my unruly hormones under control.

Blowing out a breath, I fanned my face.

I'd licked my boss' thumb.

And I wanted to lick a lot more of him.

I groaned and dropped into my desk chair. The lick, the kiss yesterday. If I wasn't careful, I was going to spontaneously combust. It had been so long since I'd had sex. Over eight months. And to be fair, sex with my ex had never been very inspiring. Scott was always more interested in Scott than me.

When I first met him, he'd seemed fine, easy-going. He'd been a fitness trainer who liked to surf.

But I found out it was mostly all a front. I was still angry at myself for not seeing it earlier. Slowly, he'd become more controlling and jealous. We'd only dated for three months, and I got tired of only doing what Scott wanted, when he wanted. And I got really tired of fast sex where usually only Scott got off.

Wrinkling my nose, I took a deep breath. When he'd hit me, it had been the final straw. I'd broken up with him then and there.

But he'd kept turning up at my work. My apartment. My grocery store. Eventually, I decided to move.

It was something I'd always wanted to do, and New Orleans had been top of my list.

So, long story short, I wanted sex. And not the boring, selfish kind. The hot, dirty, he-holds-me-down-and-gives-me-multiple-orgasms kind.

I was pretty sure it existed. I bit my lip. I was fairly certain my hot, grumpy boss was capable of it.

"No, Macy. It's a bad idea to bang your boss." I spun my chair in a circle. "No matter if you know it would totally rock your world."

"Talking to yourself?"

I yelped and nearly fell off my chair. I scrambled to my feet. Colt loomed in the doorway.

I cleared my throat. "People who talk to themselves are said to be more intelligent."

He grunted. "That sounds made up."

It probably was. I'd read it on social media.

Work. I needed to focus on some work. "I have some things for you to sign."

He crossed his arms. Did he know that made his muscles bulge? Did he do it on purpose? My gaze snagged on his tattoos. Did he have others?

"By things, you mean paperwork?" he said grumpily.

I pointed to his office. "Sit, or I'll tie you to your chair."

He stilled, and I felt the air charge. God, why did I say that? I felt a lazy throb low in my belly.

"Sit." I hope he didn't notice how high pitched my voice was. I rustled through some papers on my desk. "I'll get you a coffee." AKA a bribe.

I heard the thud of his footsteps. After sucking in a steadying breath, I headed to the kitchen and made the coffee. Colt liked his coffee black, and hot. Really hot. I had no idea why he liked it thermonuclear. Probably because he left it sitting there on his desk for so long while he pretended to do paperwork.

"I have another local case for you to look at. The details are in here." I set the file and the mug of coffee down on his desk. "Tyler Simmons. Deadbeat dad. He ran off with his wife's best friend. Original." I rolled my eyes. "He also emptied her bank account and stole her jewelry, even though they have kids." What an asshole.

Colt took a lot of cases like this. Helping out kids and single parents. I saw his jaw tighten.

"Address?"

I shook my head. "They had to sell the family home. No one's seen him since he ran. His girlfriend's address is in there."

Colt nodded.

I leaned over his shoulder. "You need to sign this form, and approve these invoices."

I realized he wasn't looking at the forms, and that his body was stiff. Oh, I was pressing my boob against his bicep. Oops. I took one step sideways.

"Why do you always smell like berries?" His voice was a low growl.

I licked my lips. "Um, it's my body wash."

Something flickered in his eyes. "You wash it all over?"

I wasn't sure that was a rhetorical question, or not, but

my brain got stuck thinking about being in a shower, and being naked, and Colt being naked.

I swallowed a whimper, but my nipples hardened. With my thin tank top, I didn't think he could miss it.

Flustered, I pointed at the forms. "Now, if you—"

I accidentally whacked his coffee mug. In slow motion, I watched it tip.

No.

I flung myself across the desk, trying to rescue the paperwork.

And managed to plant my chest in scalding-hot coffee.

Shit.

I yelped and jerked upright. "Hot. Hot. Hot."

"Macy!"

Paper flew everywhere as I tossed them out of my hand. I grabbed my sodden shirt and yanked it over my head.

I felt instant relief. "That coffee is as hot as hell."

"Are you burned?" He pulled me around, and I found myself standing between his legs.

Then his gaze locked on my chest.

I froze, doing my best deer-in-headlights impression. Today, I was wearing a candy-pink bra of sheer lace. It didn't cover much.

Colt's hands clenched on my hips.

"You wear stuff like that under your clothes every day?" His voice was deep, tortured.

"Yes," I whispered. I liked pretty underwear.

His hands moved to my waist, touching my bare skin. I moaned.

"Fuck, Macy." He shook his head. "This isn't right."

But he didn't let me go.

My blood was hot, my skin was flushed.

"You're good, nice, sweet, and I'm not."

"I'm not always sweet," I protested.

His brows drew together. "You are."

"I'm not. I can be naughty, too."

He groaned.

"And I like dirty." I frowned. "I think. I really, really want some hot, sweaty with a touch of dirty sex."

Colt groaned again. "You deserve more."

I rolled my eyes. "Women can just have sex, too, Colton Fury. Without emotions getting in the way."

"With women, there are always emotions in the way. And strings. And complications."

"That's not true."

His gaze was on my breasts, and I couldn't stop myself from arching my back a little.

He made an animalistic sound and yanked me forward.

I let out a squeak, but when his hot mouth closed over my lace-covered nipple, it turned to a long moan.

"Oh. *God.*" I slid my hands into his hair, and held him there. His tongue was magic. "Don't stop."

By the time he moved to the other nipple, I was a babbling mess.

Then he stilled.

No. *No.* I tried to say the words aloud.

That's when I heard a phone ringing.

It broke the spell.

Colt jerked back, his chest heaving. "I can't give you what you want, Macy. What you need."

I stiffened. My ex had done that. Always telling me what I should be thinking and feeling. "*I* know what I need, not you. I don't need a man telling me."

His face hardened. "Macy, you and me, we're a really bad idea."

The words hurt. I bit my lip, and fought back the painful twist in my chest. Scott had said stuff like that, too.

Bad idea, Macy. You never think.

I managed a stiff nod. “Message received.” I snatched up my sodden tank top, and went to answer the damn phone.

When I lifted it, I was barely composed and still only wearing my bra. Not to mention my panties were damp because my boss had put his mouth on my breasts. I squeezed my eyes closed. I wasn’t winning any professionalism awards today.

“Colton Fury’s office.”

There was just silence.

I lowered my voice. “Fuck you. I’ve had my limit of cowards today.” I slammed the phone down.

11

COLT

It had been a long fucking day.

I pressed my hands behind the back of my aching neck. Macy was sitting at her desk.

Ignoring me.

I closed my eyes. Every thirty seconds, all afternoon, I recalled in great detail what she'd looked like. How her sweet breasts—that were not too big and not too small—had looked, cupped by pink lace. How those tight little buds felt in my mouth.

Fuck.

About a dozen times, I'd been tempted to head over to my warehouse and jack off. But the look on her face when she'd walked out of my office had stopped me.

I'd hurt her.

I muttered a curse. I didn't want to hurt her, but I was just being honest. I came from a rocky background, and I only had room in my life for Daisy. She was my number-one priority.

In my experience, relationships never lasted. They ran

their course, or ended in violence. I growled under my breath. I was *not* thinking of my dad. The piece of scum.

I rose and walked over to the door.

Macy was at her desk. There was no smile on her face. No music playing. No origami in progress.

I'd...dimmed her light.

The desk phone rang, and she glared at it before she snatched it up.

"Colton Fury's office." She heaved a sigh. "Look, asshole, you keep up these crank calls, you'll force me to take action."

I frowned. Crank calls?

I strode over and snatched the phone out of her hand. "Who is this?"

There was silence.

But I knew the bastard was there.

"Call here again and pull this shit, and I will find you. And then you'll regret it." I set the phone down. "How many?"

Macy pursed her lips. She looked like she wanted to keep on ignoring me.

"How many calls like that, Macy?"

She shrugged a shoulder. "Half a dozen?"

"Just here? On the office line?"

She nodded.

"He calls again, tell me. I'll get Reath to work his magic."

"Sure thing, boss."

She looked at the papers on her desk like they were very important. I craned my head and saw it was a stationery order.

I wanted to apologize, but I didn't know how. And I hadn't been wrong.

Reaching over, I opened her drawer and took out a sheet of her colored paper.

She watched me, but didn't say a word.

Back in my office, I pulled out my phone and tried to ignore the fact that the paper was the same pink as Macy's sexy bra.

Soon, I was cursing my giant fingers, peering at the instructions on my phone. I sensed Macy in the doorway. When I glanced up, she stood there with her arms crossed as she watched me.

Finally, I was done. Or as done as I'd ever be.

I held the paper out. "This is for you."

She took the mangled paper, a groove forming on her forehead. "It's a...horse."

I scoffed. "It's a unicorn. I figured you'd like unicorns."

She flicked a finger at my creation. "Oh, is that what that is? I thought it was another appendage on his head. A lot of men seem to have them."

My lips quirked.

She smiled back, and suddenly my chest didn't feel so tight.

"I'm going to do some surveillance of Tyler Simmons's girlfriend." I paused. "Want to come?"

Her eyes lit up, and she clasped her hands together. "A stakeout? Definitely."

Crap. The invite had just come out unplanned. She was always saying she wanted to go on a stakeout. "It's surveillance. And trust me, it's not interesting."

"Colt, you're a kickass bounty hunter. People *all* around the country know your name. You know you have a fan group on Facebook?"

I choked. "What?"

"Ah, never mind. Let me find my shoes."

My gaze dropped to her bare feet. It wasn't uncommon for her to kick her shoes off.

I shouldn't have invited her. I needed space from the distraction of her, not to be trapped with her in a vehicle for hours. Still, seeing her light up, and talk to me, was worth it. And the paper cuts.

I grabbed my cell phone, wallet, keys, and my Nikon camera.

She was flitting around her desk. "I'm ready."

"Then let's go." I held the door open for her.

She smiled. "We're like Sherlock and Watson."

"No, we're not."

"Mulder and Scully."

I growled, heading toward my Suburban. "No."

"Bones and Booth."

"We're staying in the SUV." I opened the passenger door for her. "Surveillance only."

She tossed me a salute. "Yes, sir."

It made me picture other circumstances where she might say that. *Shit*. It was going to be a long, few hours.

It didn't take long for me to say *I told you so*.

We'd been parked two doors down the street from Simmons' girlfriend's house for almost an hour, when Macy let out another long huff.

"This is boring."

"I warned you."

She stared at the house. There was no movement. "I thought there'd be *some* action."

"Here." I held out some gum.

She shifted on the passenger seat, tucking her legs up under her as she popped some gum in her mouth. I tried not to look at her legs, or her bare feet. She'd kicked her shoes off again.

Why could the woman not keep her shoes on?

"Maybe they broke up? Or the douchebag moved onto his next victim."

"We'll see."

"Men. Why not just get a divorce before you cheat?"

"I don't cheat."

She rolled her eyes. "You'd have to have a relationship first. Why get married in the first place, and have kids, if it wasn't for him?" She shook her head. "I guess at least he wasn't abusive."

Something in her voice made me turn my head. For someone who liked to talk, she didn't talk much about her past. Had some fucker hurt her? "Someone hurt you?"

Picking up on my tone, her eyes widened. "Um, this isn't about me."

I reached over and snagged her hand. "*Macy*."

She squeezed my fingers. "You don't need to enter the overprotective zone."

"Tell me."

She fidgeted. "There was a bad ex."

"Back in San Francisco?" The fucker was a dead man.

"Yes. He was a jealous, controlling asshole. I dumped him, end of story."

"I can tell you're lying."

Her lips flattened. "Promise not to lose it?"

"No."

"Colt! I'm not telling you, otherwise."

I growled. "Fine."

"He hit me. Once. He was angry, and—"

Pure fury rushed through me. The asshole had hit her? Macy wasn't big, he could've hurt her, or worse.

"Hey, Colt, you promised."

"No, I didn't."

She slid closer, and pressed a hand to my face. "Cool it. I'm okay. I'm right here with you in this giant SUV doing boring surveillance."

"What's his name?" My words were clipped.

"I'm not telling you. Daisy can't visit her dad in jail." She stroked my beard. "It was only once. I walked out as soon as he did it, and I'd already decided I was done with him."

"And that was it?"

She fidgeted again. "Yes."

"Macy..."

"Fine. He was pushy and wouldn't leave me alone. I decided it was a good time to relocate."

My gut tightened. "He drove you out of your hometown?"

"Not exactly. It had always just been me and my mom. My dad was a bit like Tyler Simmons." She nodded her head at the house across the street. "Decided he wasn't cut out for marriage or kids. Then my mom died of cancer a few years ago, and I had no other close family. I'd been thinking about traveling for years. My mom and I always talked about wanting to do it. A big road trip adventure. It felt like my time."

I decided to do some digging and find out who the fuck this guy was.

And make sure he never came near her again.

"You aren't going to run a search on my ex," she said.

Shit. I made a noncommittal noise.

"Colt!"

"Look." I nodded at the windshield.

Macy swiveled and we watched a man coming out of the house. There was a woman in the doorway, dressed in a silky robe.

Macy gasped. She picked up the file on the center console and flicked it open. "It's Simmons."

"Yep." I watched the man pull away in a white Toyota. "Let's see where he's going."

"And bring him in." She was almost vibrating with excitement.

"Tomorrow." When she was safely not here. "It'll be a bitch to process him now. It's too late in the day."

Her shoulders slumped. "Okay."

"Afterward, I'll drop you home."

She nodded. "See, we make a pretty good team."

I wasn't a team player. My brothers and Daisy were the only people I let close.

I played better solo.

Now I just needed to remind myself and Macy of that.

12

MACY

Okay, so surveillance was boring, but tailing Tyler Simmons to a crappy motel was more interesting.

The douche had met with another woman and disappeared inside a room. How did a guy with no job, who cheated, and ignored his kids, score with these women?

I liked watching Colt do his job. The man was patient and methodical. I also enjoyed his company, even when he was grumpy.

Actually, I kinda liked the grumpy. He was honest, he didn't pretend to like something, or pretend to be someone he wasn't.

He'd dropped me home and grunted out a goodbye. I pulled leftovers out of my fridge, and stuck them in the microwave. After the stakeout, I'd changed into cutoff shorts, and a slouchy T-shirt that slid off my shoulder.

It'd been kind of cute watching Colt try to apologize to me. Not with words, but with his actions. My terrible origami unicorn was sitting on my desk at work. I leaned against my kitchen cabinet. We were attracted to each other. All too clearly, I remembered the feel of his mouth on my breasts, and I whimpered. *God*. I was slick between my legs, and I let my head drop back.

He'd made it very clear he thought we were a bad idea.

My belly did its best to tie itself in some knots. I hated that phrase. Scott had used it liberally. Usually in reference to any ideas or plans I had.

Ugh, I was *not* thinking of him. Scott Warner had sucked up more of my life than he deserved.

The microwave dinged. I pulled out my fragrant noodles and stuck a fork in. I was determined to enjoy my life. That's what my mom had done, before her life had been cut short. She hadn't done half the things on her bucket list, but she'd had a long and varied list. I admired her for that. My mom had lived life as a free spirit. Entirely her way. I was trying to do the same, and I wasn't letting anything, or anyone, get in the way of that.

And that included my gruff, sexy boss.

My overprotective boss, who was the king of mixed signals.

I chewed on a mouthful of noodles. Right, time for some extreme self-care and relaxation. Maybe I'd have a bubble bath and a glass of wine tonight? Maybe a movie? I ate another mouthful. Or read a sexy romance book in bed?

Swiveling, I pulled a bottle of white wine out of the fridge and set it on the table. A fun song came on the radio, and I boogied across the kitchen to the cabinet to get a wineglass. I'd decorated my wineglasses with these cute little tropical charms around the bases. My favorite was a hot pink flamingo, although the yellow flip flop was a close second.

Then I heard something. A thump?

I turned. It had come from the back of my house. Maybe I was imagining things?

I reached for my cellphone, then flicked off the music.

That's when I heard more noises. At my back door.

My heart exploded into action, thumping hard. I grabbed the wine bottle off the table and lifted it.

Okay, not the best weapon, but it was something. I clutched my phone in my other hand.

I walked down the hall, staring at the back door.

There was a panel of glass in the center of the wood, and I saw a shadow through it.

"Hey!" I yelled. "I see you. What the hell do you think you're doing?"

Suddenly, an arm smashed through the glass. I watched in horror as a hand reached through the gap, heading for the door handle.

Three things hit me at once. First, I couldn't breathe. Panic and fear shot through me like sludge to my system.

Second, the arm was encased entirely in black.

Three, I knew I should run, but my legs were frozen to the floor.

He pushed the handle and the door started to open. I saw a man wearing a black ski mask.

Finally, my brain and body unlocked. Pulse racing at the speed of light, I screamed and threw the wine bottle.

I heard him grunt and duck. As the bottle smashed, I whirled and ran.

I sprinted through the kitchen. I hit the corner of the cabinet with my hip, and pain burst along my side.

Get somewhere safe. That was all I could think.

I heard footsteps. He was coming after me.

My heart was in my throat as I raced into my bedroom and slammed the door shut. I flipped the lock, but I was very conscious that it was flimsy. I sucked in some harsh breaths.

Not enough. Not enough.

I moved to my lovely wooden dresser that I'd found in a great little secondhand store. I heaved. It moved several inches across the floor.

The door handle rattled.

Fuck a duck. I bit my lip and tasted blood. I shoved with everything I had.

I didn't want to die.

I didn't want to end up on a Netflix documentary as the victim of a serial killer.

The dresser moved in front of the door, just as a heavy weight hit it. I stared wide-eyed, listening as the door rattled again under another heavy blow.

Swiveling, I glanced at my windows. They had pretty bars on them that I'd liked when I'd moved in. They were safe. Secure.

Now I was trapped by them.

Help. I needed help.

I fumbled my phone, my hand shaking. I stabbed at the screen.

It rang. And rang.

"Come on," I whispered.

"Macy?" Colt's deep voice was the best thing I'd ever heard.

"Oh my God, Colt! He broke in!"

"What?" Colt barked. "Who?"

"I don't know. A man just broke down my back door and chased me." My voice broke. "I'm trapped in my bedroom. I got my dresser in front of the door."

The bedroom door was hit by a heavy weight again. I heard wood crack.

I whimpered. "He's trying to get in."

Colt cursed. "Hold on, Macy. I'm coming." I heard him yelling something to someone. "Hold on, baby, I'm coming."

I gripped my phone. I already felt better knowing he was coming.

"Stay on the line, Macy."

"Okay, Colt." I heaved in a breath, and heard the roar of an engine across the line.

My bedroom door vibrated again. To my horror, I saw my dresser start to move an inch.

"Oh, God, Colt." I dropped the phone and lunged for the dresser.

13

COLT

"Macy! Macy!" As I sped toward Macy's house, the line went dead.

I gripped the wheel and stomped on the accelerator.

If someone hurt her...

I wrenched the wheel and sped up. I had to reach her.

Reaching out, I stabbed at the dash.

"Colt?" Reath's voice. "Everything all right?"

"No. Macy called, and someone broke into her place. The bastard's trying to ram down her bedroom door."

"Fuck. Address?"

I rattled it off. "I'm on my way there."

"I'll meet you. Colt, don't do anything stupid."

I pressed my lips together. In my job, I hunted down some terrible people. Rapists, murderers, torturers. I was known for being ice cold. I always put my emotions on ice on the job, and channeled them into the hunt.

But I'd seen what sick men could do to women.

Hold the fuck on, Macy.

I took another corner, my wheels screeching.

I was almost there.

Finally, I jerked to a halt in front of her place.

It looked undisturbed. There were lights on, and jaunty potted plants with red flowers out front on her tiny porch.

A red McLaren 650S Spider screeched to a halt, and Reath sliced out. He was in a suit, so he'd probably been at a meeting with a client.

My brother nodded, and pulled out a Smith and Wesson handgun. Reath always used a different gun, so he'd never get too used to one model. My SIG was in the back of my waistband.

We reached the front door. Reath tried the handle, but it was locked. He pulled out a lock pick.

I really didn't like the fact that it took him less than twenty seconds to pick Macy's lock. She needed better locks.

As we walked inside, the neat living area was quiet. It was totally Macy. A comfy couch, wildly colored pillows, bright art on the wall. I saw colored paper on the coffee table and half made origami in process. The glass bowl in the center was filled with origami flowers.

Reath raised his weapon. I followed, clearing the rooms as we went.

I saw the back door wide open. There was smashed glass on the floor and what smelled like white wine.

Reath straightened. "Clear."

Whirling, I faced the final closed door. I saw the dents on it. Someone had kicked it.

"Macy!" I roared.

"Colt?" Her voice was muffled by the wood. "Oh, thank God."

There was the sound of feminine grunting, then scraping. The bedroom door flew open.

And there she stood. Unhurt. Her legs and feet were

bare, her loose T-shirt had slipped off one shoulder. Her curly hair was a little wild.

I strode to her and lifted her off her feet. She wrapped her arms and legs around me, clinging hard.

I buried my face in her hair.

"I was so scared," she said.

"I've got you. You're safe now."

She shuddered against me, and I vowed that I wouldn't stop until I found who'd terrified her. I breathed her in. That scent of berries.

"I've got you." I set her down, cupped her face, then tipped it up. "Are you all right?"

She nodded and managed a small smile. "I am now."

"Good." I stroked her cheeks with my thumbs.

"Glad you're okay, Macy."

She glanced at Reath and nodded. "Thanks for coming." She looked back at me. "And for being so fast."

"He came in the back?" Reath asked.

Macy nodded, then lifted her chin and glanced around. "You're sure he's gone?"

I saw her shiver and slid an arm around her. "He's gone."

We reached the back door, and she swallowed. It was clear he'd broken the glass and reached inside.

Reath crouched, careful not to touch anything. "There's a wine bottle here."

"Oh, um, that was me. I threw it at him."

I stilled. "You threw it at him? Instead of running?"

"I wasn't really thinking clearly, Colt. I was afraid. I ran afterward."

Jesus. If he'd gotten his hands on her...

"You didn't recognize him?" Reath rose.

"No. He was dressed all in black, with a ski mask and gloves."

"We probably won't find anything, but I'll get my guy to look for prints. And I'll report this to the police."

She wrapped her arms around her middle. "Right."

I pulled her closer. "Pack a bag."

"What?"

"It's not safe here. We need to get your door fixed, and new locks." And a state-of-the-art security system. And I wanted whoever had broken in behind bars before she came back.

"I don't have anywhere to go. I..." She looked around, and I could tell she really didn't want to stay.

"You do." I cupped her shoulders. "You're staying with me. I'll make sure you're safe."

Her lips parted. Over her head, I saw Reath not bothering to hide his smile.

"Go," I urged. "Get some things."

With a nod, she headed for her bedroom.

I looked at my brother. "Find whoever did this, Reath. Before I do."

14

MACY

"You can sleep in my bedroom, Macy."

I smiled down at Daisy. She was so sweet, especially in her Wonder Woman pajamas. Adorable.

"Thanks, Daisy. Your dad put my bag in the guest room at his place."

Colt had a kickass, renovated warehouse. I'd only gotten a glimpse of it, but it rocked the industrial vibe with brick walls and concrete floors. He didn't have much furniture, though. It had a very spare, empty look that was less Scandi style and more ascetic monk. It said "man lives here," which was the complete opposite look to the adjoining house we were currently in.

I knew the Fury brothers owned this entire block of the Warehouse District. They had their own warehouses and businesses, but this house in the center was a home. It was done in light, airy tones, with a huge couch and large kitchen. There were loads of pretty house plants, which I assumed were thanks to Lola. I knew for a fact Colt wouldn't keep a plant alive. Daisy's room was upstairs, and

Lola's. The building was connected to Colt's warehouse, and was within easy reach for the other brothers.

My brain suddenly did a U-turn, reliving watching that arm reaching through the broken door, the man in black coming after me.

My heart started pounding again, and a wave of dizziness washed over me. I knew I was breathing too fast. I stumbled to the couch and dropped down.

"Macy? Daddy, something's wrong with Macy."

The couch dipped. I felt the big body beside me, and strong hands cupped my face.

"Macy, look at me."

I did. I loved looking at that masculine face, and those blue eyes that made me think of the palest sea glass.

"Breathe," he ordered.

I pulled in some air.

"There you go. Good girl. Slow it down." His thumb stroked along my cheekbones. "You're safe. Say it."

"I'm...safe."

With his solid, secure presence beside me, I felt the fear and panic recede. Daisy pushed into my other side, burrowing into me.

I fought a smile. Surrounded by father and daughter, both doing their best to comfort me. I stroked a hand over Daisy's hair. "I'm feeling better now." I met Colt's gaze. "Thanks."

He nodded. When he shifted away, I felt the loss of his body acutely.

"Dai, time for bed."

The little girl's head jerked up. "But—"

"I know it's exciting having Macy here, but she'll be here in the morning. Bedtime."

"But Daddy—"

"Daisy." His tone turned firm.

I found this fascinating. Colt in dad mode.

The little girl huffed out a breath. "Fine."

I hid a smile. Seven going on seventeen.

"Say good night to Macy."

"Night, Macy." Daisy threw her arms around my neck. "Have a good sleep. My daddy will be right beside you. He'll keep you safe."

My eyes flew to Colt.

"Right beside you in the bedroom next to yours," he clarified.

"Of course." I squeezed Daisy. "Thanks, gorgeous girl."

Colt and Daisy headed out, her smaller hand engulfed by one of his big ones. So stinking cute.

I sagged back on the comfy couch and wrapped my arms around myself. I knew the crime in New Orleans was bad. The man who'd broken into my place must have just been some opportunistic thief. He hadn't been expecting me to be home.

I nibbled my lip. Except that my lights had been on.

The creepy phone calls popped into my head. And my magically moving mug.

I shivered.

Colt returned, scowling at his cellphone.

"Is everything all right?" I asked.

"I just got a message from Reath. He's on his way over."

A sense of impending doom wound around me. "Why?"

"He has something."

Colt started to pace.

A minute later, Reath walked in. I only saw him because I was facing the doorway. The man moved silently. He'd ditched his suit jacket and rolled up the sleeves of his white shirt. I was too nervous to process that the look really worked for him.

His dark gaze flicked to me before he looked back at Colt.

"Oh, God." I pressed my hands to my stomach. "You know who it is. Did I narrowly avoid being murdered by a serial killer?"

Reath crossed his arms. "There was a doorbell camera on the neighboring house that caught a glimpse of him. Like you said, he was wearing a mask. We can't get any facial recognition."

"Okay," I said slowly.

"We could tell that he's about six feet tall, athletic build, white."

Colt scowled. "That doesn't narrow it down much."

"I did a bit more digging." Now Reath looked at me.

Reath Fury was very handsome, like hard-to-look-away handsome. He had beautiful, brown skin, along with short, black hair, and lips that gave a girl ideas.

But right now, he looked a little scary. There was this look in his eye...

"I want to talk about Scott Warner."

My heart sank.

Colt straightened. "Who?"

"Her ex, who she reported to the police in San Francisco for controlling, stalking behavior."

A thunderous look crossed Colt's face. "The fuckhead who hit you?"

I swallowed. "Scott is my past, and I prefer not to talk about him."

Reath and Colt just stared at me.

"You think this was Scott?" Dread solidified in my chest. "But he's in San Francisco."

"He was fired from his personal training job three weeks ago," Reath said. "For harassing women."

I twisted my hands together. "I've been gone for over six months. I only dated him for three months. Honestly, only the first few weeks were any good. I thought he was a nice, easy-going guy."

"Until he showed his true colors." Colt sounded like he was talking through barbed wire.

"Yes." I pushed my hair back, feeling so tired. "He slowly turned controlling. He was always angry at everything I did, jealous. Nothing I did was right. He gaslit me constantly." I sucked in a sharp breath.

"What?" Colt said.

"The other day, my favorite coffee mug moved in my home. I *always* put in the same place. It was missing and I found it on my table, with the handle broken." I felt the color leech from my face. "He knew I loved that mug. My mother gave it to me. And I've been getting prank calls at the office. No one ever talks. And I got a weird delivery. A stack of empty boxes."

Colt cursed and strode to the bank of windows, his hands pressed to the back of his neck. "He was the one that knocked you off your bike."

I felt like I was going to be sick.

"We don't know for sure if all of this is Warner," Reath said. "But I'll look into him. Confirm if he's in New Orleans."

"It's been months," I said.

Reath met my gaze. "How did he take the breakup?"

I fidgeted. "Not great."

Colt whirled. "We need to know everything, Macy."

I blew out a long breath. "He hit me. A closed fist to the cheek. I was lucky he didn't break it."

Colt made a deep, angry sound. "And he only hit you once?"

"Just once. I dumped him right then. But afterward, he turned up at my apartment, at work, followed me at the shops. He'd yell or cry, plead with me to take him back."

Reath's face hardened. "I'll get my team working on this straight away. Macy, don't worry, we're going to help Colt keep you safe."

With a nod at the both of us, Reath left.

Colt was tense. He looked like he was about to snap, or explode.

"Colt?"

"He punched you in the face."

"Once."

"You should've told me how bad it was."

"It's in the past." I shot to my feet. "I don't focus on the past, or fixate on the negative. My mom always said to look to the future. To look to the good things."

"It's not the past if Warner is coming after you. It's stupid to ignore the warning signs and waltz around like life is all fucking rainbows and love hearts."

My hands balled. "I'm *not* stupid. He used to say that. *You're not very bright, Macy. You've always got your head in the clouds, Macy.*"

Colt's face darkened. "Do not compare me to that asshole."

"Then stop acting like him. This is not my fault, Colton Fury. I didn't ask for this." My anger exploded like paint bombs inside me. I snatched a pillow off the couch and threw it at him.

It bounced off his chest.

Then I swiveled and stalked out. I found the door

leading to Colt's warehouse, wrenched it open, and marched right to the guest room where he'd put my bag.

I slammed the door closed behind me.

It was satisfying for about three seconds, then tears welled in my eyes.

I felt afraid, angry, hurt.

Wrapping my arms around myself, I sat on the bed.

And now, like always, alone.

15

COLT

I stared out the windows. The brick warehouses outside were a blur. Lights were on in the small office tower. It was Kavner's. He lived in the penthouse, and the rest of the building was filled with offices for his business empire.

I pinched the bridge of my nose. I'd lost my temper. I hated when I did. It reminded me too much of my father.

Just the thought of Macy in danger, getting hit...

My hands flexed.

I'd find Scott Warner. And if he wasn't the guy, I'd keep searching until Macy was safe.

There'd be no more fucking panic attacks.

And no more losing it and making her feel worse.

As I was trying to teach Daisy, when you messed up, you apologized. I stomped through my warehouse. It was usually my sanctuary. Or my bear cave, as my brothers liked to call it. Today, it didn't make me feel better.

I reached the guest room and stopped. I stared at the door for a few minutes before I finally found the courage to knock.

"Go away." Her voice was muffled.

"Can I come in for just a minute, Macy? Please."

Through the door, I heard her huff. "One minute is all you get, Colton Fury."

I shook my head. Macy was incapable of staying mad at anybody for very long. It was probably why she'd lasted so long as my office manager. I frowned. Assistant.

Pushing open the door, I saw her in the center of the bed, her knees tucked under her chin. She looked small and sad. My heart shriveled. This was my fault.

I looked at the wall. "I'm...sorry."

"Why?"

I looked at her. "Because I upset you."

"That's not why you should be sorry, Colt."

With a sigh, I walked over and sat on the bed. "I lost it. Ran my mouth off. I was worried, but I don't think you're stupid. You're the opposite of stupid."

She just stared at me with big, sad eyes.

I blew out a breath. "My dad killed my mom."

Macy gasped and launched forward. She grabbed my arm. "*Colt*. I'm so sorry."

"Neither of them were particularly good people, but my mom didn't deserve to die." Shit, my skin itched. I hated thinking of those days, let alone talking about it. I never talked about it. "I was there when it happened. We lived in a trailer." Old and dirty were the best two adjectives I had for that place. "My parents argued a lot. Usually when they were drunk or high."

Her small hand stroked my back. It eased some of the pressure in my chest. I'd come in here to comfort her, and now she was comforting me.

"The last time, my dad lost it." I closed my eyes. "They were shouting, throwing things. I hid in my closet." I'd listened to the shouts and the screams escalate. "I didn't help her."

"How old were you?"

"Nine."

"You were a *boy*. There was nothing you could have done."

I made a sound.

"Colt." She pressed in closer. "Would you expect Daisy to stop a fight between two brawling adults?"

Horror filled me. "No."

She arched a brow.

Scraping a hand through my hair, I blew out a breath. "He went to jail."

"And you went into the system."

"Yeah. Then years later, I found out that my father had another child. With his prison-bride pen pal. She was one of those people who fall in love with inmates. They had a daughter. Chrissy."

"Daisy's mom."

I nodded. "Chrissy didn't have much stability. My dad was absent, obviously. And her mom was a flake. I connected with Chrissy when she was almost sixteen. She was already using drugs."

"You tried to help her."

"I took her to rehab so many times." I gripped my thighs. I had so many fucking regrets where my sister was concerned. "When she was clean, she was amazing. Funny, caring, with a wicked sense of humor." I'd had a sister. A blood family member who actually gave a shit about me. "Then, she went off the rails again."

Macy's hand slid up to the back of my neck and squeezed.

"I was trying to get her to go back to rehab, but she told

me I was bossy, always in her business." That wasn't even close to the vile shit Chrissy had spewed. I knew it had been the drugs talking, but it still hurt. "So finally I left her alone. I decided to wait until she came to me and asked for help."

Macy leaned her head against my shoulder, and I smelled berries.

"She never did." My tone was flat, devoid of emotion. "She ODed. She'd managed to get clean for a while when she was pregnant with Daisy. She had no idea who the father was. But even after holding that amazing life she'd made in her hands, the demons got to her." I paused. "I failed her."

"No," Macy said strongly.

"Shouldn't have given up."

"No, Colt." She pulled my face to the side to look at her. "You can't help someone who doesn't want your help. You did everything you could."

I covered her hand with mine. "You have to let me help you."

"I will." Her hands tightened on my cheeks. "I promise."

"You can't get hurt, Macy."

"I won't."

My gaze dropped to her plump lips. She was so close. I could smell her, see those freckles on her skin, feel the press of her against me.

Shit. "I don't do relationships. I can't. Daisy is my number one priority, and nothing comes before her."

"You could never fail that little girl. You love her, and she loves you."

I pulled Macy closer until her breasts were against my arm. My cock stood up and took notice.

This close, I could see the desire in her eyes.

"*Colt.*" A low whisper.

I felt something snap inside me. She'd been chased, frightened, could've been hurt. I could have lost her. This chance could have been snatched away.

I slammed my mouth against hers.

She made a hungry sound, her hands sliding into my hair.

Damn, she tasted sweet. I swept my tongue into her mouth. I wanted to explore every part of her. Memorize her taste.

Her T-shirt had slipped off one shoulder, which was driving me crazy. I leaned down and scraped my teeth over those maddening freckles.

"Colt. *God.*"

I tumbled her back on the bed. Her blonde hair was everywhere, her face flushed with need. I palmed her breasts, thumbed her nipples.

With a moan, she pushed into my hands. "I love your hands," she panted. "*Please.*"

Macy was in need. And it was like I was programmed to give this woman everything she needed.

"You hurting, Macy?" My voice was a low growl.

"*Yes.*"

"Where?"

Her eyes flashed. "Everywhere." She paused. "Between my legs."

With a growl, I flicked her shorts open and yanked them down her legs.

She only wore a tiny scrap of black lace beneath them. "You call these panties? These things are designed to tease me." I slid a finger under the elastic. She writhed.

I pushed her thighs wide, and lowered my head. The scent of her lush arousal hit me. I scraped my mouth over her lace-covered pussy. "Been wondering if you had curls here or kept it bare."

Her teeth sank into her bottom lip. "Find out."

I growled, and shoved the gusset of her panties aside. Bare and smooth. I stroked her.

"*Oh.*" She arched off the bed.

"You're soaked. Wet for me already. Panties soaked. Pussy soaked." I caressed her slick folds.

"*Colt.*"

I loved the tremor in her voice. I gripped the lace and with one hard yank, ripped her panties off her. Now she was completely bare for me.

"So smooth." I stroked my thumb up and found her clit. She moaned sweetly for me.

I had to taste her. I pushed her thighs wide, lowered my head, and feasted.

She cried out and tried to rear up. Holding her still, I tongued her folds. So damn sweet.

"Oh, Colt." Her hands tugged on my hair. She was close and I wanted to taste her release.

There was a tentative knock on the door. "Daddy? Are you there? Your bed's empty. I'm thirsty."

I froze, and beneath me Macy stilled.

Fuck. The universe was giving me a big reminder why I didn't get involved, and didn't bring women home.

Macy was trembling, on the verge of coming.

I tried to clear the lump in my throat. "Be there in a second, short stuff." She usually went to Lola. I suspected the excitement of Macy being here had gotten too much for her.

She wasn't the only one.

Shit, what the hell was I doing?

I stood, and readjusted my aching cock that was bulging in my jeans.

Macy watched me, then closed her eyes and pulled in a shuddering breath. Her body was trembling.

"Macy..."

"Go." She flicked the cover over her body.

Should never have touched her. I wasn't built for this.

"Just go," she whispered.

I needed to take care of my kid.

I needed to keep Macy safe.

And I needed to keep my dick in my pants and my hands to myself.

I turned and stalked out.

16

MACY

I woke in a comfortable bed looking at a concrete ceiling crossed with black metal beams. I blinked, and remembered where I was. Colt's.

A second later, I remembered everything that had happened.

Ugh. I was pretty sure being almost abducted and then having my grumpy boss almost get me off were not the kind of adventures my mother recommended.

I sat up, and pushed my mass of tangled hair back. I'd slept pretty well, considering. Probably thanks to the orgasm I'd given myself. I closed my eyes, and pictured in great detail just how great Colton's dark head had looked between my legs.

His mouth had felt even better.

I flopped back down on the pillows. I had no idea what level of grumpiness I'd find today. I'm sure Colt would be back to giving me his "no relationship" speech.

Well, shit was going down in my life, and I really, really wanted the distraction of some hot sex with multiple orgasms.

With Colt.

He could give me that. And I knew a part of him wanted to.

What if it screws up your job, Macy?

Sleeping with the boss was not a good idea. Well, once he was done with me, I'd move on. Find the next adventure. My mom had always said to live life to the fullest.

Life's full of adventures, Macy Moo. You just have to find them all. Don't let anyone, especially a man, hold you down.

Maybe Colt would be an adventure. For however long it lasted. Mom had always drummed into me that nothing lasted forever.

My stomach rumbled. Shower, food, and coffee. That was all I needed right now.

I took a quick shower. I loved the rain shower head in the huge shower in the bathroom. Pure decadence. In my head, I decorated the industrial-style bathroom, with its gray tiles and wall of weathered wood, with some much needed pops of color. Some teal-colored towels. A jeweled toothbrush holder. Maybe a plant.

I dug out some clothes from my bag. After a quick shake, my pretty, yellow sundress would do. It was Saturday, the sun was shining, and I was safe. It felt like a sundress kind of day.

I was determined to focus on the good stuff.

When I wandered through to the main house, I smelled coffee and bacon cooking, and heard Daisy's infectious giggle.

I stepped into the sun-drenched room, and my gaze cut straight to Colt. My mouth went dry. He was standing at the stove, cooking in jeans, and a burgundy T-shirt. The sleeves were tight, cutting into his biceps.

I licked my lips. Why did the man have to look so good?

"Macy!" Daisy's cry made me jolt.

Colt's head whipped around. When his gaze dropped, skimming over my dress, I felt my body temperature skyrocket.

"Morning." There, that sounded relatively normal.

Daisy bounced on her stool at the island. "Daddy's making pancakes. His pancakes are soooo good."

"Oh, I love pancakes."

"I know." Colt's tone was gruff.

"Daddy said you needed pancakes."

I felt a flush of warmth. "Thank you."

"Coffee is fresh." He tilted his head toward the pot.

I ruffled Daisy's hair and circled the island. As I passed Colt, he shifted, his body brushing mine.

My pulse went crazy. His hand brushed my hip, squeezed.

"I like the dress." Then he stepped back to the stove.

Trying to calm the raging butterflies in my belly, I headed for the coffee pot. Mmm, it smelled good.

Then I stumbled to a halt.

My favorite mug was sitting on the counter, with the handle glued back on. Tears pricked my eyes, and I sucked in a breath.

For a man who didn't do relationships, he was pretty good at them.

"Macy? Are you okay?"

I turned my head and smiled at him. "Yes." After pouring my coffee, I topped it off with creamer.

"You know, why bother with the coffee at all? Why don't you just have a mug of creamer?"

I poked my tongue out at him and rejoined Daisy at the island.

As she ate her pancakes, the little girl babbled about her best friend, Leah, who had a dog called Milo. Apparently, Milo was the best dog in the world and could do tricks.

"Aren't dogs great, Daddy?" She shot him a pleading look that I imagined was designed to hit every parent right where it hurt.

Colt grunted.

I took pity on him. "School starts soon."

Daisy's nose scrunched. "In a few days." Her tone was resigned. "Our teachers have a few days at school without us, then we go back."

"Then you get to see your friends every day."

The little girl's face brightened, and she smiled. "I hope Leah is in my class."

"Good morning."

I jolted and almost spilled coffee down my dress. I swiveled on my stool and glared at Reath. "I'm getting you a bell to wear around your neck. To warn everyone when you're coming. You just about gave me a heart attack."

A small smile crossed his face, and again, I stared at his handsome features.

Then reality crept in. Why was Reath here on a Saturday morning? I swallowed, my throat thick.

"Dai, go find Lola," Colt said. "You can play on the tablet for a bit."

"Yay!" She was gone like a bullet.

I set my coffee mug down. "You found Scott."

"Not exactly," Reath said, setting a black backpack down.

A big hand took mine and I looked up at Colt.

"You're not alone, Macy."

"I've been alone a long time. Since my mom died." I

found a smile, but it was hard. "But it's okay. It makes it easy for me to move around, explore, find new adventures."

Colt's scowl deepened a notch. "You're not moving around. You live in New Orleans now. And you're not alone." He looked at his brother. "Tell us."

"Scott Warner flew into New Orleans a week ago."

I gasped. "So it was him. The calls, my mug, the attack. God, he'd been in my place! And he knocked me off my bike." I jumped off the stool and started pacing. I threw my arms up. "Why? Why can't he just hear my no? I'm not interested."

"Because he's a selfish, narcissistic fuckhead who likes getting his own way," Colt said.

"Hell yes, he is," I agreed.

"I have a contact in San Francisco," Reath said. "He owns a security company over there, and I asked him to do some digging on Warner."

My stomach felt like I'd swallowed rocks. Reath pulled a sleek, black laptop out of his backpack and set it up on the island.

Colt gestured to a stool, and I sat. Reath sat beside me, while Colt stood at my back.

The screen came to life as the video call connected, and a man appeared.

Oh, wow. I hadn't met any men like him when I lived in San Francisco. He wore a suit, but I got the distinct impression he should be in battle gear, directing warriors as they headed into battle. He had a good-looking face, bronze skin, and dark eyes. He kind of emanated a dangerous vibe that made me swallow.

"Hi, Vander," Reath said.

On screen, the man nodded. "Reath. Colt."

"Vander, this is Macy," Reath said. "Macy, this is Vander Norcross."

I lifted a hand. "Hi."

Vander nodded. His dark gaze was a little hard, like there was nothing that he hadn't seen. I realized his eyes were actually dark blue.

"Sorry to hear about your troubles, Macy." He had a deep voice. "Sounds like this Warner is a piece of work. He was fired from his job at the gym here in San Francisco, and he wasn't happy about it. He left several ranting messages on the gym's social media pages. He also kept turning up at the gym after he was fired, was rude to the customers."

I clutched my hands in my lap and swallowed. *God.*

"The gym owner said Warner was harassing women. They'd had several complaints. I sent Saxon—" Vander looked at me again "—he's one of my men, to talk to some of the women." Vander's mouth tightened. "They all had the same story. Warner seemed nice at first. Charming, easy-going, but became more aggressive and controlling. Wouldn't take no for an answer."

"That sounds like Scott," I said.

Vander's gaze met mine, and my pulse jumped until Colt put a hand on my shoulder. The touch steadied me.

"Scott Warner is not a good guy, Macy," Vander said.

"I should have seen it sooner."

"That's not on you," Vander said.

I bit my lip and nodded. Colt's fingers squeezed my shoulder.

"Saxon also talked to a few guys Warner worked with at the gym. Apparently, he talked a lot about his girlfriend. The one he wasn't going to let get away."

I pressed a palm to my churning belly. Colt growled, and I reached up with my other hand and put it over his.

"Warner got violent with Macy," Colt said.

Vander's face sharpened. "You guys better stop him."

His tone said that otherwise he would.

"We're on it, Vander," Reath said.

Colt squeezed again. "The bastard isn't getting close to Macy again."

Vander nodded. "If you need any help, Boone is in town."

I wondered who Boone was. I figured if he knew Vander and the Fury brothers, he was another badass.

Reath leaned forward. "He's a long way from his farm in Vermont."

"He was working a personal protection job for me for a businessman from Shreveport. He's just finishing up, and has a few days in New Orleans. You'd be doing me a favor if you'd check in with him. Spends most of his time on that farm alone, with only his dog for company."

Reath smiled. "I seem to remember you used to be a bit of a loner, Vander. Before you fell for your police detective."

I cocked my head, sensing a story.

Vander made a sound. "My family wouldn't let me be a loner. My mother is Italian-American, and always up in our business. But yes, having my lovely detective has given me a new perspective." His lips tipped up.

Wow. I wondered what kind of woman captured the heart of a man like Vander Norcross.

"But Boone doesn't have family or a woman," Vander continued. "I'm worried about him, and a few others who served with me."

"We'll give Boone a call," Colt said.

Vander inclined his head. "Thanks. And good luck teaching Warner a lesson."

Reath touched the keyboard and ended the video call. "

"I'm going to find Warner and stop him." Colt's tone was low and dangerous.

I froze. "Stop him meaning put him in jail?"

A muscle ticked in Colt's jaw. "Meaning whatever it takes."

I jumped off the stool and grabbed his arms. "But nothing illegal. You have a daughter, big guy, and...and I'm not bringing paperwork to jail for you to sign."

Reath made an amused sound.

Colt cupped my cheek. "It's going to be all right, Macy."

I relaxed.

"But I will do whatever it takes to stop Warner."

I tensed again. I'd been alone for years since my mom died. I was used to depending on myself. I wasn't used to trusting someone else, having someone put themself out there for me.

"You'll be careful," I ordered.

Colt just stared at me. "Whatever it takes."

17

COLT

As I walked into Hard Burn, I strode straight past the boxing rings and the people training in them.

I saw a small crowd watching the main ring and headed that way.

I'd left Macy, Daisy, and Lola making cookies in the kitchen. Macy and Daisy had been giggling, heads together.

My girls having fun. I scowled and almost missed a step. I meant my girl and Macy having fun.

My hands flexed. Last night, having her laid out for me, and my mouth on her pussy...

My cock throbbed and I cursed.

It couldn't happen. I needed to keep my eye on the prize—keeping Macy safe, not on how many orgasms I could wring out of her. She was such a responsive little thing, greedy.

Fucking hell. I couldn't risk failing her. Shaking my head, I looked at the boxing ring and focused on Beau and Kav who were sparring.

Beau was big and solid. He was shirtless, his tattoos and rock-hard chest and arms on display. His shaggy, black hair was damp with sweat. Beau was a bulldozer. He kept going, and never stopped until he won. He'd been the same in his teens, in the military, and in his decade as a mercenary.

Anyone would hesitate to go up against him.

Except Kavner.

Kav was tall and lean. He had a long, elegant body to go with his good looks. But the gloss covered grit. I knew how Kav had grown up, what he'd endured in the hellish crucible of his childhood.

And no one became a billionaire without smarts, hard work, and determination.

Kav was also shirtless, his skin more golden than Beau's. They were both slicked with perspiration.

Beau charged, and Kav dodged his punches. They traded blows, grunts filling the air. Beau was more powerful, but Kav was faster. And he used it to his advantage.

He whirled around Beau, and landed a hard punch to Beau's lower back. With a growl, Beau shifted, feinted, then landed a heavy uppercut to Kav's gut.

With a curse, Kav hit the ropes. But he knew how to take a hit. His tailored suits hadn't changed that. He slid sideways and went at Beau again.

I moved to the ropes. "Beau, I need a minute."

"Let me finish wiping the floor with Kavner."

Kav snorted. "I haven't been anywhere near the floor, old man."

They traded a few more punches, then pulled up.

Kav stretched his neck, then gently touched his stomach. "Damn you for hitting like a freight train."

"Need to move faster." Beau grabbed a towel and slid through the ropes. "How's Macy?"

"Fine. She's bounced back." I glared at the wall. It was

covered in framed boxing photos. "She's making cookies with Lola and Daisy."

"Cozy." Kav appeared, chugging back some water.

I squinted at the bottle. It was some sort of fancy Italian stuff. "Regular water not good enough for you?"

Kav smiled. "No." He paused. "So, it's her ex who's doing the harassing?"

My shoulders tightened. "Looks that way. Reath called Vander Norcross to follow up on what this asshole was doing while he was in San Francisco. Turns out he was an asshole to other women too." A muscle in my jaw ticked. "But he considers Macy his. The one who got away."

Kav cursed. "He's escalating."

"Yeah. Reath is trying to track him down. I've made a few calls to my contacts to keep an eye out for him, but the guy isn't from New Orleans, so it won't be easy to find him." My usual tricks for finding people included visiting friends and family, or surveilling people's usual hangouts. I couldn't do that with Warner. I turned to Beau. "The guy's a PT. Thought you could put out feelers. I figured he might want to find a local gym to work out."

Beau nodded. "Good idea. I'll call around."

"I'll get you the asshole's picture." I dragged in a breath.

Kav slapped my shoulder. "We've got your back. We're not letting Macy get hurt."

I nodded. "How about a family dinner tonight? To take Macy's mind off things. Unless you've got some fancy-ass date at some fancy-ass restaurant."

"Or a meeting," Beau said. "Kav's always got a meeting."

Kavner smiled. "Money doesn't make itself, gentleman. I happen to take care of all your investments, and make a lot of money for you in the process."

Kav had a brilliant, sharp brain. Thanks to him, I had a hell of a nest egg, and money for Daisy's education. "All right, see you both later."

"You think he realizes he's gone over his pretty office manager?" Kav asked Beau, his expression smug.

"Nope," Beau answered. "He's too stubborn to admit it. Needs to spend some time in denial first."

I stiffened. "I only have room in my life for Daisy. And Macy is my office *assistant*."

Kav laughed, low and smooth. "Funny how he keeps repeating these things, like if he does it enough, they'll actually become the truth."

Ignoring them, I turned and walked out.

18

MACY

"Then Colt proceeded to drink the entire pack of beer to prove Beau wrong," Reath said.

Perched on my stool at the island, I grinned. "Then what happened?"

"He puked everywhere in the garden. Got his first taste of a hangover at fifteen."

I laughed and looked at Colt standing beside me, holding a beer. He was scowling at his brother.

His gaze dropped to me, or more accurately to my mouth, and his scowl softened. "Never drank Budweiser again."

I reached for a corn chip and dunked it in the guacamole. It was the best guac I'd ever tasted. Once again, Lola was the queen of good food.

The queen was currently moving around the large kitchen, humming to herself. She was making jambalaya, and it smelled so good. My mouth was watering.

Daisy was doing a craft on the rug in front of the television. She was studiously gluing feathers and sequins onto a glass jar. We hadn't told Colt that it was the infamous swear jar. He'd find out soon enough.

Beau was sprawled in a chair at the huge table with Reath. We were waiting for Kavner, Dante, and Mila to arrive.

"Let's see what other embarrassing stories I have about teenage Colton." Reath tapped a finger against his lips.

"Stop it," Colt growled. "Or I'll share some stories about you."

Reath just smiled. "I'm an angel."

Beau snorted. "That's the biggest lie I've ever heard. You're just good at not getting caught."

"Who's lying?" Kav sauntered in.

I blinked. It was the first time I'd seen the billionaire in jeans. They fit him perfectly, and he wore them with a blue button-down that made his eyes stand out.

He was carrying a white box in his hands.

"I brought dessert." He whirled into the kitchen and kissed Lola's cheek. "To give this lovely woman a bit of a break."

"You bought it, right?" Lola asked. "You didn't bake."

"Lola, are you insinuating that my cooking skills are lacking?"

"Yes," his brothers all echoed together.

Kav pressed a hand to his heart. "I'm wounded."

He didn't look wounded.

"I also thought the lovely Macy deserved something sweet." He winked at me.

I smiled, just as Colt clamped a hand on my shoulder. When I looked up, he was scowling at Kavner. "Well, I love dessert. As long as there's no coconut. I'm allergic."

"No coconut in sight. It's Amaretto cheesecake from Angelo Brocato."

Beau swiveled. "Fuck, I love their cheesecake."

"Uncle Beau!" Daisy piped up, proving young ears always heard what you didn't want them to hear.

"Add it to my swear jar tab, Dai," Beau said.

"No wine?" Colt asked Kav.

"No. Dante's bringing some new local whiskey that's he's started stocking at the club. Mila said she'd make cocktails."

"Where are they?" Beau asked.

Reath snorted. "I don't need three guesses to know what's held them up."

Sure enough, five minutes later, the couple appeared.

"Sorry we're late." Mila Clifton hurried in, bags in hand. "We got sidetracked."

Since Mila's cheeks were flushed, and her brown-gold hair was sporting a style commonly known as sex hair, it was pretty easy to guess where that sidetrack had taken them.

Dante followed her; he had a sort of a prowl that made a woman give him a look or three. He had dark hair, a short, dark beard, and right now, a satisfied smile.

"I'm going to make cocktails." Mila set the bags down on the island and started pulling out bottles.

Dante tugged her hair. "Once a bartender, always a bartender."

I'd heard about some of Mila's troubles. She'd overheard something criminal and shady at her old job, which had put her in danger. She'd ended up on the run, and gotten a job as a bartender at Dante's club.

And ended up in Dante's arms and in love.

I sipped my beer and watched the pair. Dante looked at Mila like she was precious.

Mila caught his look and smiled. He dropped a kiss to her shoulder.

My belly did a funny flip-flop. Yep, I was jealous as hell. Having a man like Dante Fury clearly adore you... I fiddled with the label on my bottle, and because I couldn't stop myself, I glanced at Colt.

My heart jolted. He was looking at me.

"It was a hot one today." Mila opened a bottle of whiskey. "We'll probably get a storm later." She expertly started mixing the cocktails.

"No flaming cocktails?" Reath asked.

Mila smiled. "Not tonight."

Dante's club, Ember, specialized in flaming cocktails.

"Mila's Smoked Cinnamon is already incredibly popular." Dante leaned against the island, pride in his voice.

"Macy, would you like a cocktail?" Mila asked. "Sounds like you've earned one lately."

"I'm not a girl to say no to a cocktail. I'd love one."

A moment later, Mila handed me a glass. She passed others around, and we all tried Mila's creation. She'd also made mocktail versions for Lola and Daisy.

It was delicious, and I happily gulped the cocktail down.

Soon, Lola corralled everyone to the table, and I enjoyed the good food, good drinks, and good conversation. There was no end of banter and teasing from the men. I felt a warm glow. I'd never had this. A big family gathering. A sense of being part of a tight-knit group.

It had just been mom and me. It'd been wonderful, but I hadn't realized until now that maybe we'd been missing out on something. That having people, laying down roots, wasn't necessarily a bad thing.

"Okay?" Colt slid an arm across the back of my chair.

I breathed in his citrus-lime scent and nodded. I felt him toy with my hair as he turned to keep talking with Kav.

"They can be a hit to the senses."

I glanced at Mila who was sitting on the other side of me.

"You've got that right."

Mila smiled, but it faded. "I'm sorry to hear about your ex causing you trouble."

My good mood soured a little. "Thanks. I'm hoping he loses interest soon."

She touched my hand. "You can trust Colt, and his brothers. They all had my back." She looked over at Dante and I saw love in her eyes. "Ending up here was the best thing that happened to me."

"I'm glad for you, Mila."

She squeezed my fingers. "You'll get there, too." She looked at Colt. "I mean, you'll be safe."

I nodded.

"Daddy, can we go in the pool?" Daisy asked.

"Pool?" I loved to swim. "I didn't know you had a pool."

"There's one on the rooftop of Colt's warehouse," Reath said.

"Maybe later, short stuff," Colt told his daughter.

Lola rose from her chair. "Let's have dessert, before we do anything else."

I sat there, absorbing it all. The camaraderie, Daisy's funny comments, the warmth of Colt's body close to mine.

I knew it wouldn't last. Life changed constantly, people came and went. But I would enjoy it while I could.

19

COLT

"Okay, thanks, Matt. If you come across anything else, let me know."

Ending the call, I leaned back in my office chair. It was Monday morning. Daisy was out shopping for new shoes with Lola. I was chasing some leads on Scott Warner.

I flicked through my cell phone until I reached a photo of the fucker. He was smiling, buff in that way you got in the gym. He was good-looking, and I hated that. I bet the guy couldn't win a fight to save his life.

Maybe the only time he liked swinging a punch was at a woman half his size.

I heard Macy out in the front office on the phone. She sounded happy. We'd had a quiet Sunday. We'd taken Daisy to the aquarium. My girl loved fish. I knew if she couldn't con me into a dog, she'd switch to begging for a fish.

Despite the simmering tension both Macy and I worked hard to ignore, it had been nice, the three of us out. Daisy holding our hands.

Don't get used to it, Fury.

I had to stay focused on my daughter.

I rubbed the center of my chest. I also had to stay focused on hunting down Scott Warner.

So far, I wasn't winning. Scott hadn't used his credit card, and was lying low like the snake he was. I'd put out feelers, and Reath was looking. Beau was asking around the local gyms.

The asshole would pop up somewhere, and I'd be ready when he did.

In the meantime, it was taking all my control to keep my hands off Macy. Being so close to her was torture, whether we were at the aquarium, watching TV with Daisy, or grilling steaks for dinner.

I'd managed to ignore her sunshiny laugh, her bare legs, and her painted toenails for all of Sunday. I blew out a breath. I just had to keep it that way.

"Hey." She wandered in, flicking through some papers in her hand. "I have a couple of jobs for you to look over, and a Detective Broussard called while you were on the phone. He said for you to give him a call back when you can."

Broussard was a cop friend. I took the papers from her.

She fidgeted a little.

"What's wrong?"

She touched her hair. "Nothing."

"Macy, just spit it out."

"Any news on Scott?" She whirled away. "A part of me doesn't want to know. If I just ignore him, it's like he doesn't exist." She whirled back, her hands waving in the air. "But I know I can't do that. I have to face my problems." Her shoulders slumped.

"Don't cry," I growled.

"I'm not." Her voice sounded watery.

"I don't want to have to make more origami."

That got a laugh out of her.

"We don't have anything on him yet. Don't worry."

"Colt, that is impossible. Anxiety is alive and well over here, trust me."

I grabbed her arm and pulled her onto my lap. She made a cute squeak, and I tightened my arms around her.

"What are you doing?" she asked.

"Giving you a hug."

"Oh?"

"To help you relax. You're safe."

"Oh." Slowly, she relaxed into me. "I bet you hug Daisy like this. I bet she thinks nothing bad will ever happen to her because you're her dad."

"Nothing bad will ever happen to her."

Macy traced the tattoos on my forearms. That small touch seared through me.

"Bad things will happen, Colt. You can't stop that. And you can't feel guilty about it, either. All you can do is be there for her."

I grunted, my chest tight.

"You can love her, be there to help her put the pieces back together. My mom used to say we aren't to blame for the bad stuff that happens in our lives, but we are in charge of healing from it."

"Sounds like a wise woman."

"She was."

Macy snuggled deeper against me, and my cock swelled. *Shit.* I counted to ten, trying to find some control.

She stilled, then the little minx moved her ass. Deliberately.

I gripped her hip. "Macy."

"Yes, Colt?" Her voice was breathy.

She knew exactly what she was doing. She was in

another fucking dress today. It was flirty. White with blue stripes. Summer personified.

I had no right to touch something so sweet.

"You're going to get up now." I gripped her knee. Her skin was so smooth.

"Okay."

Neither of us moved.

She deserved some nice guy, who could buy her flowers every day and didn't swear all the time, and who could give her a damn white picket fence.

I slid my hand up higher, and heard her breath hitch. Her dress had a deep *V* neckline, and I could see the swells of her pretty breasts.

My cock was harder than steel now.

"Colt, I know you said you don't do relationships. I understand, sort of. And I promise, I'll keep all my strings and complications to myself."

I gently stroked her inner thigh and she jolted. "Macy—"

She gripped my wrist. "I want you to touch me. I want to know what good sex is like. Really good sex, with lots of orgasms. Sex that's a little rough, a little wild."

Fuck me.

The fact was, I wanted to give this woman everything. Everything she wanted. Everything she deserved.

But I was pretty sure that wasn't me. With my scarred hands, my rough demeanor, and a life full of fuck-ups.

Then she murmured my name, and moved my hand until it brushed her silky panties.

Fuck it. A man could only hold out so long. I tipped her head back and kissed her.

As my tongue dominated her mouth, I pushed her

panties aside and stroked her. She moaned into my mouth, grinding her ass against me.

I stroked her pussy roughly. "My girl's wet for me."

"*Yes*. Colt, yes."

My cock had never been harder. I thrust my fingers inside her, and she tilted her hips to give me better access.

"You wear these dresses to tempt me, don't you? To make me want to slide my hand up here." I stretched my fingers inside her.

She made a choked sound. "Don't stop."

My thumb found her slick clit, and I massaged her, watching her face. I quickly worked out exactly what she liked best. I felt her tensing up, her breaths coming in fast pants.

"Colt..."

My phone started ringing. Her eyes went wide.

I knew she was worried I'd leave her hanging again. Not this time.

I ignored the phone and pinched her clit. She was trembling, and I heard my pulse thudding in my head.

More than anything, I wanted to watch her come. Steal all that sweetness for myself.

"*Colt*," she gasped.

"Come for me, Macy."

She did. I kept touching her pussy, watching the pleasure take her. Pleasure I gave her.

She cried out, her thighs clamping closed around my hand. I held her as her body shuddered, emotions flitting across her face. Beautiful.

Finally, she slumped back against me, a dazed look on her face. "*Wow*."

I kissed the side of her head and breathed in the aroma

of her arousal mixed with berries. Slowly, I pulled my hand free, and she bit her lip. She shifted, and I bit off a curse.

I was about to come in my damn jeans.

"Colt—"

My cellphone rang again. I pressed a kiss to her temple and snatched it up. Beau's name was on the screen.

"Beau."

"Colt. I just got a call from a buddy. He owns a mixed martial arts gym out in Bucktown. He just saw your guy walk in like he was the king of New Orleans."

I stiffened. I saw the light leak from Macy's face.

"Thanks, Beau."

"Need me to come with you?"

"I'll be fine. Thanks." I stood, set Macy on her feet, and took a second to smooth the skirt of her dress down. "I have to go."

"What's wrong?" She gripped my arm.

"Someone just spotted Warner."

20

COLT

When I pulled into the industrial area in Bucktown, I scanned around. The gym was in a long, rectangular building, divided up for various businesses. I saw several cars parked outside the MMA gym, that had a red sign above the door with a logo of two gloved hands.

I watched one man exit the gym, carrying a bag over his shoulder. I really hoped Warner was here, so I could finally get Macy safe, and stop her worrying.

As I'd left the office, I'd called Reath to keep an eye on her. His security team was only a few doors away, and he had a camera at the front of my office.

I parked my Suburban, turned off the engine and waited. Lots of my job involved waiting. Watching, waiting for my prey to make mistakes so I could nab them. I'd learned to be still and quiet as a kid, while my parents were high, partying, or fighting. My hands flexed on the steering wheel. I was doing everything in my power to ensure Daisy never, ever had to be still and quiet, simmering in her fear.

More people came and went from the gym. None were Warner.

In my head, I relived touching Macy in my office. She was so responsive. Every sound and move she made was burned into my brain.

I want to know what good sex is like. Really good sex with lots of orgasms. Sex that's a little rough, a little wild.

I groaned. I wanted to give her that. And I sure as hell didn't want anyone else touching her.

"Focus on finding Warner first," I muttered.

First, I needed her safe.

Shoving the door open, I sliced out of my SUV and headed toward the gym. It was a hot, humid day. Typical for New Orleans. A teenager with earbuds in slunk past me, head down, and backpack over one shoulder.

As I neared the gym door, a gun shot rang out.

Chips of concrete hit my legs as the bullet hit near my feet. Then I was moving. There were more shots, bullets hitting the building behind me.

I dived, and rolled, and slid in behind a parked truck. I glanced back, but the teenager was out of sight. Thank fuck.

More gunfire. I heard it hitting the truck body, and glass shattered.

Where are you, asshole? It sounded like whoever had the gun was firing from a distance.

More bullets pinged on the vehicle I was using for cover. I listened, gauging the direction.

I pulled my SIG, and waited for a pause. Then I popped up and fired.

Bam. Bam.

I ducked back down. There was another barrage of gunfire, then silence.

I smiled grimly. I'd spooked him.

Whoever my shooter was, he was a shit shot.

I heard the screech of tires and peered over the hood of

the truck. I spotted a silver car speeding out of the lot. Sedan. Too far away for me to catch the plates.

The door of the gym flew open.

"You okay, man?" A guy in a polo shirt with the gym logo stood there, worry on his face.

I rose, and tucked my handgun back into the holster at the small of my back. "Yeah."

"I called the cops."

"Thanks." I saw worried people crowded in the doorway. "The shooter took off. You're safe."

"Jesus." The gym worker thrust a hand through his hair.

"Have you seen this guy?" I held up my phone with the picture of Warner on it.

The man's brow creased. "Yeah, he was in here earlier. Asking about memberships. Real blowhard. Kept saying how good he was in the ring. He left, but I saw him hanging around outside for a bit."

My mouth flattened. The fucker had lured me here. He'd seen me move Macy into my place, and he wasn't happy about it.

Luckily for me, Warner was a crappy shooter. He was pissed, and he'd lured me here. Why? To scare me? To make a point?

As I headed for my SUV, I saw a piece of paper fluttering under my wiper blade. I stiffened.

I yanked it out and my gut tightened.

It was a picture of Macy sitting at her desk in my office. It had been taken through the front windows. She was leaning one elbow on her desk, smiling, the phone to her ear.

Someone had scrawled *Mine* across the picture.

I scanned around. Warner had clearly paid the teenager

to leave this while he took shots at me. My heart lodged in my throat. I yanked my phone out and hit Reath's number.

"Colt?"

"Someone took a shot at me outside the gym where Warner was spotted."

My brother cursed.

"I'm fine. He couldn't hit a paper bag if he was inside the bag. Left a photo of Macy on my SUV. Her at the office."

Reath cursed again. "Hang on."

"Get over there, Reath. He—"

"She's fine. I have eyes on her on my security feed."

My racing pulse slowed a notch. "You sure?"

"Looks like she's singing."

My head dropped forward. "She does that. A lot."

"Wait, someone's headed in. Don't worry, it's a woman, not Warner."

"Okay." I saw a patrol car pull in. "Cops are here. I'll give a statement and then head straight back. Watch her for me."

"You got it, Colt."

21

MACY

My fingers tapped on the keyboard as I finished some emails. My foot tapped the floor.

Was Colt okay? Had he found Scott?

I picked up some paperwork, then set it back down. I was too churned up to be very effective. I pressed my fingers to my forehead.

What was wrong with Scott that he'd stalk a woman who wasn't interested in him across the country? He needed help.

Colt would be fine. They didn't come any more badass than my bounty hunter.

My heart flip-flopped. My bounty hunter? It wasn't true, but I wanted it to be. The way he'd touched me in his office, had made me come, I wanted more.

I shivered. He thought he didn't do relationships, but he was already taking care of me. And he was an amazing dad.

You promised him no complications, Macy.

The front door opened and I jerked my head up. When I saw it wasn't Colt, my shoulders sagged.

A woman sauntered in, looking around with interest.

The first thing that came to mind was biker babe. She was tall, curvy, with jeans that were long past too tight. Her white tank hugged her large breasts and she had big, brown hair. She looked a few years older than me, but it was hard to tell because she was wearing a lot of makeup.

"Hi, can I help you?"

"So this is Colton's office. Wow." She did a slow circle. That's when I noted she was carrying a small container.

"Ah, yes. Did you want to make an appointment?"

"Oh, I just really wanted to see him and give him a gift." The woman touched her tongue to her lip.

My stomach did a weird turn. Was this an ex? "Do you know Colt?"

"I'm his *biggest* fan. I'm Marsha. I'm head of his online fan club."

I blinked. I'd teased Colt about his fan club, but I hadn't expected to meet the head of it.

"We all just *love* bounty hunters. Big, strong men who track down criminals." Marsha gave an exaggerated shiver. "Doesn't hurt that the man is gorgeous with a very big G." She winked. "And I'm sure other things are big too."

Sitting back in my chair, I kept watching the woman. She was a groupie. In love with the image, but had no idea what the real man was like. She had no idea that he was dedicated, a good dad, a loyal brother, protective.

"Well, Colt's out, so I'll let him know you stopped by, Marsha."

The woman's gaze narrowed a little. "You can't have him."

"Excuse me?"

"Little thing like you isn't enough woman for a man like Colton Fury." She tossed her hair back over her shoulder.

"You don't even know Colt past his photo. Look, it's time for you to leave."

I saw a bunch of emotions cross Marsha's face, too fast for me to tell exactly what she was thinking.

Finally, she blew out a breath and smiled. It wasn't a real one. "Sorry, I just... I'm obsessed with Colton. I just know he's a good guy. I didn't mean to be a bitch."

I softened a little. Colt was enough to go to any woman's head. "Okay."

"Here." She set the plastic container down on my desk and pulled off the lid. "I made these brownies for him. But you try one. As an apology."

"Okay." I had to admit the brownies looked good. "All right, fine." I took a piece of chocolatey goodness. I bit in and raised my brows. It tasted good. The woman was smiling at me. "These are great."

Marsha's smile widened. She looked very pleased with herself. "You give the rest to Colton, now. Bye." She sauntered out, denim-clad hips swaying.

Shaking my head, I turned back to the computer. There was still no word from Colt.

He will be fine, Macy.

A few minutes passed. I scratched my forearm, then scratched again. I hated when I got dry skin. Actually, I was thirsty too. Rising, I headed to the kitchen for some water.

When I reached for a glass, I wheezed. Frowning, I swallowed and rubbed my chest. My throat also felt thick.

I staggered. I felt weird. It was hard to breathe.

Oh, no.

I pushed off the counter, clawing at the neckline of my shirt. I saw the rash on my arms.

Shit. Allergic reaction. It had been a really long time

since I'd had one. My gaze flew to the brownies. Oh hell, was there coconut in there?

Shit. Shit. *Shit.* I stumbled. I used to carry an EpiPen, but when I moved, it had expired. I hadn't gotten around to replacing it. I mean, it was pretty easy to avoid coconut. And who put it in brownies? I hadn't seen any.

Sit down, Macy. Don't panic.

I tried to walk, but I toppled and fell on the floor. I whimpered. My breathing really labored now.

Oh my God. I couldn't die from coconut. Life couldn't be that unfair.

I dragged myself out of the kitchen and toward the desk. I needed to call 9-1-1. I needed to hit the panic button. I needed help.

The room spun and I whimpered.

I kept crawling. My breathing was just a wheeze now and my dizziness was growing.

Oh, God. Please, please someone help me.

22

COLT

I didn't waste any time getting back to the office. I'd given my statement to the New Orleans PD, leaving out the part about knowing Scott Warner was behind the shooting.

I'd deal with the fucker myself.

Right now, I wanted to get back to Macy.

I pulled into the back of the warehouse, then headed around to the office. Maybe I'd take Macy out for lunch.

Daisy had a sleepover at her best friend's house tonight. My gut tightened. That meant it would just be Macy and me at home. I glanced up. Storm clouds were building. The humidity was reaching uncomfortable levels. We'd get a storm soon.

When I opened the office door, I found it empty. I frowned. "Macy?"

I heard a noise. A choked sound.

Surging forward, I rounded her desk and saw her sprawled on the floor.

"Macy!"

I dropped to my knees and rolled her over. Her breathing was a harsh, labored rasp. Her face was flushed, and I saw panic in her eyes. Her neck was covered in a rash.

"What happened? *Fuck.*"

She tried to talk, but just touched her throat. She was having trouble breathing.

"Baby, tell me what you need?" I fumbled to get my phone out, holding her tightly. I stabbed at the screen. "Reath! Macy's down. She can't breathe. It looks like a reaction to something."

"Fuck," my brother bit out. "I'm on my way."

Heart racing, I stroked her hair. "I've got you, Macy. Hold on." Her gaze locked on mine. I touched her cheek. I hated that wheezing sound of her breath. "That's it. Focus on me."

I felt her tense body relax a little, but I could see panic in her eyes.

"A-a-llergic."

"Okay. Stay calm. I'll never let anything happen to you."

Reath burst through the door, a first aid kit in his hand. The one he kept at Phoenix Security Services was better stocked than a hospital. He took one glance at Macy and his jaw tightened. "Anaphylaxis."

I nodded.

Reath put the kit on the desk and ripped it open. He pulled out an EpiPen and handed it to me.

I yanked the lid off, then jammed the pen against Macy's thigh.

She jolted.

"There, Macy. You'll be fine now." I handed the empty pen to Reath, then pulled her onto my lap.

She buried her face against my shirt.

Soon, I felt her body relax.

"Thank you." She sounded a little hoarse, but her breathing was already better.

I felt jittery myself, seeing her like that. I pulled her closer. "What happened?"

"This woman came in. Marsha." Macy's nose wrinkled. "She's head of your online fan club."

"My what?"

Macy's lips twitched. "She's a groupie. A bounty hunter groupie."

I grunted.

"Anyway, she was rude—"

My fingers tightened. "How?"

"It doesn't matter. She offered me a brownie. She'd made some for you." Macy waved a hand at her desk. "There must be coconut in there. I'm allergic."

Reath picked up the container and sniffed. "I don't see or smell coconut."

"I know. It's weird. I always check."

Something in me stilled.

"She must've used coconut oil or something," Macy said.

"Is that common in brownies?" I asked.

Her brow creased. "I don't think so."

"Warner know you're allergic?"

Her mouth dropped open. "Yes."

Reath cursed. "Colt, I'm sorry. I saw the woman leave and Macy looked fine. When she headed into the kitchen, she was out of view, and I didn't know anything was wrong."

I nodded. "Reath, find that woman. I want her questioned."

Reath nodded. "You got it, Colt." He glanced at Macy. "She should go to the hospital."

She shook her head. "No. I'm fine."

"It's standard after using an EpiPen," Reath said.

Macy clung to me. "I don't want to go. I really don't like hospitals."

I smoothed a hand down her hair. "Call Doc Hamilton. I'll have her check Macy."

"I'm all right—"

I scowled at her. "It's not up for discussion."

Her face pinched. "Colt—"

I gripped her chin. "You're getting checked. *Fuck.*" I dropped my forehead to hers. I'd dropped the fucking ball. She could've died. If I'd been a few minutes later...

"Colt, I'm okay." She kneaded my shoulders. "Look at me."

I met her green gaze.

"I'm *fine.*"

I nodded. "You're still getting checked out."

She eyed me for a second. "Okay."

I was pretty sure she was humoring me. I rose with her in my arms, and set her in her desk chair.

"Doc's on the way," Reath said, slipping his cellphone away. "Sorry, Colt. I didn't think that woman was a threat." Reath's jaw was tight. "I won't underestimate Warner again."

"I didn't think Warner would hurt Macy. This is my fuck up."

Reath's face hardened. "He's continuing to escalate."

Macy had almost died.

Emotion wrapped around my throat, squeezing tight. I turned and punched the wall. I left a hole in the drywall. Behind me, Macy gasped.

I punched it again.

Reath grabbed my arm. "Dial it down, Colt." His voice was a low murmur.

"She nearly died."

"She's fine. Right now, she needs you to take care of her, not lose your shit."

My body vibrated.

"Got a lock on it?" Reath asked.

I blew out a breath and nodded.

"Take it out on Warner."

"Find him, Reath."

"I will. He's not going to get to her."

"No, because he has to go through me, first."

23

MACY

"You're going to be fine, young lady. But you need to get this script for an EpiPen filled."

The handsome, older black woman handed me the piece of paper. Her dark hair, shot through with gray, was in a bob around her face.

"I will. Thanks, Dr. Hamilton."

The woman smiled. "It's my pleasure." She lowered her voice and glanced at Colt. "I think you'll have a tougher time calming him down."

We were in Colt's warehouse. He was pacing back and forth by the kitchen island. He hadn't stopped since the doctor had arrived.

"Goodbye, Colton," Dr. Hamilton said breezily.

He lifted his head. "Thanks, Doc. You sure she's okay?"

"She's fine. I'll send you my bill."

"Reath has you on retainer."

"So he does." She walked past him and squeezed his arm. "Your girl is going to be just fine. Say hi to Daisy from me. I'll see myself out."

With another nod, the doctor headed for the stairs.

I pushed my hair behind my ears and watched him. "Colt?"

He kept pacing. "You need something? A drink. Snack?"

I rose. "I could do with a hug."

He jerked. "I'm not really known for my hugs."

"I bet Daisy would beg to differ." I walked over to him and wrapped my arms around his middle. He was so hard, and I listened to the comforting, solid beat of his heart.

He was still for a moment, then wrapped his arms around me. I breathed him in, and felt my tension lowering. But I could still feel his.

"I won't let Warner get you, Macy."

"I know. My allergic reaction is not your fault."

His hands flexed on me. "If I'd been a bit later getting back—"

"Shh." I slid my hands under his shirt and up his back. "I'm fine." We stayed like that for a moment. "I take it you didn't find Scott."

"Not exactly."

I knew that evasive tone. I pulled back and looked at him. "What happened?"

"Nothing." His face was blank.

"Colt."

He sighed. "When I reached the gym, someone took a shot at me."

I blinked. "A shot at you?" My heart squeezed. "Like they tried to punch you?"

"No, like with a gun."

My chest locked. "He shot at you!"

"Macy, calm d—"

I threw my hands in the air. "That crazy asshole tried to kill you!" I shook my head, my anger building. "I did nothing but try to like him, and in return I get *this*. And now he's targeting you, as well?"

"Macy." Colt clamped his hands on my arms. "Take a breath."

I looked at his handsome face. It wasn't classically handsome, it was a little too rough around the edges, but it looked perfect to me.

God. What if Scott had managed to shoot Colt?

I pulled in a shaky breath. Colt was looking after me, and I wouldn't let Scott hurt him.

"Hey, whatever is going on in that head of yours, stop it."

"Colt..." I just needed to escape all this for a bit. From the look of Colt's Level 5 scowl and tense shoulders, so did he. "Can we go somewhere? Where there is no Scott? No bullets? Just... Get away for a bit?"

He looked at me for a beat, then nodded. He took my hand and towed me toward the stairs. "Get changed. You'll need jeans or long pants."

"Okay."

I ducked into the guest room and pulled on my favorite navy-blue leggings, and a pretty, off-the-shoulder blouse in white.

Colt was waiting for me. We headed down to the ground floor garage.

"What about Daisy?"

He didn't respond, just staring at my bare shoulders.

"Colt?"

He grunted. "She's at her best friend's house for a sleepover."

"Oh." So it was just the two of us. Alone.

When the lights clicked on in the garage, he didn't head

for his SUV, his big truck, or the fancy black muscle car that looked tough and growly.

"I have something for you."

I glanced up at him. "Really?"

He pointed.

I saw my bike leaning against the wall. In perfect condition. My mouth dropped open. "My bike." I rushed over and touched the front wheel. There was no sign it had ever been damaged. "You fixed it."

He slid his hands into his pockets. "I know you love it. Even though it's a ridiculous color."

"It is not." I felt like I was melting inside. There was some pretty ribbon in a teal and pink tied onto my basket. I touched it and lifted a brow.

Colt cleared his throat. "Daisy added that."

"Thank you."

He nodded.

"Are we going for a bicycle ride, then?"

He snorted. "No."

No, I supposed badass, grumpy bounty hunters did not ride bicycles.

He led me farther into the garage and that's when I saw the motorcycle. My pulse jumped. A big, tough-looking motorcycle. A Harley.

"We're going for a ride on that?" I breathed.

He glanced sideways and his lips quirked. "Yeah. You like bikes?"

"I've never been on a motorcycle, but I've always wanted to."

He pulled a helmet off a hook on the wall. "Here."

I put it on, and he helped me adjust the straps. Then he pulled his own on. He climbed onto the bike, and my belly did a weird tumble. He looked so hot.

"Hop on." He patted the seat behind him.

I swung my leg over and settled behind him on the leather.

"Hold on tight." He pulled my arms around him.

I rested my hands against his flat stomach and my cheek against his back. Oh, I liked this, and it had nothing to do with the bike.

He started the engine. It was loud and grumbly, vibrating through my body. I grinned. It reminded me a lot of Colt.

Then I held on, as he pulled out of the warehouse.

Wherever he took me, I knew it would be just where we both needed to be.

24

COLT

I followed Route 18 out of the city, running parallel to the Mississippi River.

I kept checking for a tail, but when I was sure there was no one following us, I relaxed a little.

The city gave way to countryside, and soon it was all swamps and plantations. Every time we caught a glimpse of a stately plantation home nestled amongst old trees, Macy would pinch me.

I found myself smiling. It was like taking Daisy somewhere. Her excitement was infectious.

Although what I felt for Macy was nothing like what I felt for my daughter.

My tension drained away as we passed sugar cane fields and levees, shacks and country churches. I turned south, and we passed through small towns and bayous. There was so much history here, imbued in the landscape—from the slaves who'd survived here to the Cajun and Creole culture.

Memories of my earliest years bubbled up. I'd been born in a town like the ones we were passing. But with Macy snuggled up against me, for once, I didn't remember the bad times, the fights, or the times I went hungry. This time I remembered running wild with my friends, fishing, catching crawfish.

I pulled over on the side of the road so we could drink some water and stretch our legs.

Macy hopped off the bike. "I want a Harley."

My gut cramped as I handed her a water bottle from the saddlebag on my bike. Macy riding a Harley alone was not happening.

"You ride with me."

Smiling, she took a big drink of water. "Did you see those plantation homes? They looked like wedding cakes dotted across the fields. And the cypress trees. They're just so...stately and giant."

I shook my head and drank my own water. But as my gaze drifted upward, I noted that dark storm clouds were growing on the horizon. A thunderstorm was coming. I wanted to get Macy home before it hit.

"Let's keep moving."

Soon, with Macy holding me tight, we were back on the road. Before long, we headed back into New Orleans. The fields gave way to houses and shops.

I felt steadier. Having Macy pressed against my back had helped. She was safe and alive. I'd do whatever I had to in order to keep her that way.

The clouds continued to build. *Fuck.* We wouldn't make it home.

I'd barely finished that thought when the heavens opened.

We were soaked in an instant. Macy squeezed me. As we stopped at some traffic lights, I glanced back.

She was laughing. Her white shirt was transparent and

sticking to her skin, and she had her face tipped up to the sky.

My gut clenched so tight that it hurt. I'd never met anyone like Macy before. Someone who just enjoyed life, smiled, charged through anything negative, and found the good. She was like a sunflower, always following the sun.

She was like a firefly darting around and I wanted to hold her in my hand, and never let her go.

I just fucking wanted her.

The light changed, and I gripped the handlebars. As we reached the Warehouse District, the rain finally started to ease, the storm moving off to drench somebody else.

The brief reprieve from the humidity was over though, and I could feel it building again.

Or maybe it was just the raging desire inside me.

I reached my warehouse and thumbed the remote in my pocket. The garage door slid open. As I drove inside, the Harley's engine echoed in the cavernous confines. I stopped the bike and shut off the engine. As I climbed off, the need inside me felt like the storm. Powerful, unstoppable. I pulled my helmet off.

"That was *amazing*. The ride, the scenery, the storm." She was still sitting on the bike, face flushed, mouth smiling. She pulled her helmet off, shaking her damp hair out.

Beautiful. She was temptation in a perfect package. My pulse was pounding in my head. I dropped my helmet, and it clattered on the concrete floor.

She jerked and her gaze flew to my face. Her smile disappeared. "Colt?"

I took her helmet and tossed it too. My gaze dropped to her shirt. It was completely see-through. I could see her lacy, white bra underneath, the dark smudges of her nipples. Reaching out, I cupped one breast.

Her lips parted.

"Had these pressing into my back the entire time, teasing me."

She made a hungry, husky sound and pushed into my touch.

"Now this shirt isn't hiding anything. These pretty tits are begging me to touch them. Suck them."

"Yes. *Please.*"

She sounded far too sweet, begging me. I liked it. My cock was already harder than it had ever been. I pushed the neckline of her shirt down, then the cups of her bra. Her breasts popped free, pink nipples already hard.

I groaned. Beautiful breasts, beautiful nipples. "Baby, look how pretty you are." I leaned down, and sucked one nipple into my mouth.

Whatever she moaned, I couldn't make it out. All I could hear was her need. She wriggled, her hands plunging into my hair.

"I love your beard scraping my skin. I love your mouth on me."

"You love me sucking these pretty tits, sunflower?"

She moaned. "*Yes.*"

I moved to the other breast. Need was a hard beat inside me now. There was no way I could stay away from Macy. If I didn't find out what it felt like to slide my cock deep inside her, I wouldn't survive.

Pulling my mouth off her plump breast wasn't easy. Straightening, I shoved her back to lie along the curved seat of my bike.

Pure beauty.

Quickly, I yanked her leggings and panties off.

Oh no, now this was pure beauty. A near-naked Macy on my bike.

I gripped one slim calf, sliding my hand up her skin. Then my gaze locked on the sweet pussy that I'd uncovered.

I needed to suck in air and grit my teeth to stop from coming.

I pushed her legs apart and pressed my face between her thighs.

Fuck. She tasted like spicy honey. I dragged my tongue over her, absorbing her cries.

Time to make my girl come.

25

MACY

"Oh...*please*."

Colt knew exactly what he was doing with that mouth of his. As he licked me, desire twisted inside, leaving me shaking.

It was too much, and not enough.

I looked down at the decadent picture we made. Me, practically naked, laid out on his Harley like a sacrifice.

A very willing one.

And Colt's head buried between my thighs. He looked up the length of my body, and everything inside me clenched. The dark, hungry look in his eyes, his mouth on me...

When his teeth scraped over my clit, I bucked.

One of his hands flattened against my belly, holding me still for the relentless pleasure his mouth was giving me.

"Colt... I need..." My voice was coming in pants.

"You need to come for me, Macy."

It was like he'd opened the floodgates. My orgasm hit me like a hurricane. It swept through me, hot pleasure inundating me.

Everything inside me spasmed, and as my body shuddered, Colt held me in place. Kept me safe.

I rocked against his mouth, husky sounds escaping me.

Oh, my fucking God. I wanted him. I wanted his big, hard body naked, fucking me, his cock inside me.

Colt lifted his head, and nibbled my inner thigh. My chest was heaving.

He helped me sit up, then one big hand was in my hair, pulling my head back. His mouth wasn't gentle. The kiss was hot, fierce, his tongue owning my mouth. I tasted myself on his lips.

"Not done yet, sunflower." He lifted me off the bike. My bra and shirt were shoved down to my waist. He quickly pulled them off.

"Okay?" he asked.

Hell, no. I felt like I'd just barely survived a wild storm. But I managed a nod.

"Good." Then his hands closed around my waist, he lifted me, and threw me over his shoulder.

"Colt!"

"Be good, sunflower."

"Maybe I don't want to be good."

As he headed toward the stairs, his palm cracked against my bare ass. I cried out.

"Like that, baby?" He stroked between my legs and I bit my lip. "You're so nice and wet for me."

Then he jogged up the stairs, carrying me like I weighed nothing. It was hot. So hot. I mean, I knew I wasn't big, but I wasn't tiny, either.

A second later, he strode into his bedroom.

It had an airy, industrial look. A large bed with a metal and wood frame rested against a white-washed brick wall. The bed was covered in a pale gray bedspread. Black metal accents crossed the wall, and a modern light hung from the ceiling. Apart from the bed, there was no other furniture.

He dropped me on the bed, and I bounced once.

Then he pressed his hands to the mattress on either side of me and looked down. He was breathing hard, his muscles strained.

"Colt?"

"I want you so fucking much. I'm afraid I'll hurt you." His pale blue gaze hit mine. The intensity seared me. "I'm big, rough... You're small, with soft skin, you're too sweet."

My pulse went crazy. "You could never hurt me, Colt. And I'm not too sweet. I want a little rough, a little wild, remember?" I licked my lips and lowered my voice. "I need it."

He just stared at me, and my skin felt flushed, itchy. I needed this man to touch me. I just had to convince him.

"Give me your hand."

He hesitated for a second, then sat beside me, the bed dipping. He held out his big hand.

I took it in mine, trying not to focus on the fact that I was naked, and he was still wearing his storm-wet clothes.

I traced his palm. He had such long fingers. It wasn't the hand of a man who sat at a desk all day. It was strong, weathered, with calluses.

But I'd seen those same hands be gentle, with his daughter, with me.

His scent curled around me—that lime undertone that I suspected was his soap or shower gel. I highly doubted Colt wore cologne. Added to it was the smell of the storm.

I lowered my head and pressed a kiss to his knuckles. I felt his gaze on me—a hot, heavy weight. Then, I lifted his hand and licked the tip of one finger.

He made a low, masculine sound. I sucked his finger into my mouth, the next sound he made was grittier.

I saw desire burning in his eyes. For me. This man wanted me so much. I sucked his finger deep. This time he growled my name, and fed a second finger between my lips.

I sucked harder and he pushed deeper until I gagged a little. When he tried to pull back, I gripped his thick wrist.

"You sure this is what you want, sunflower?"

I nodded.

He pulled his fingers free and gripped my jaw. "Say it. Out loud."

"Yes, Colt."

"Tell me what you want, Macy." His chest rose and fell.

"You. I want you."

With a curse, he yanked me onto his lap, his hands sinking into my damp hair. He pulled my head back, exposing my throat. I gasped.

Then he raked his teeth over my neck. "Then you'll take everything I give you."

26

COLT

Twisting my hands in Macy's hair, I pulled her mouth to mine.

I swallowed her moan, crushing those soft lips as I devoured her. I was so damn hungry for this woman. This bright ray of light.

As I stroked her tongue with mine, absorbing the warm, sweet taste of her, I felt my desire amping up.

Obsession, protectiveness, need. It was all twisted up inside me.

For Macy.

Gripping my shoulders, she broke the kiss. Her breath panted against my lips and undulated against me. "No one's ever kissed me like that before. Like I was needed."

I squeezed her hips and she ground against my throbbing cock. She let her head fall back, all that beauty on display. She had a long neck, pretty breasts, flat stomach, and that bare pussy rubbing against my jeans.

Fuck.

I pressed my mouth back to her neck and sucked. She

moaned my name, her hands flexing on my shoulders. Then she gripped my T-shirt.

"Off. *Please.*" She was breathless.

I ripped the shirt over my head. Before I could do anything else, her hands attacked the fly of my jeans.

My growl was loud and guttural. When she freed my cock, I'd never been harder. She stroked me, and her lips parted.

"Harder," I demanded.

She stroked harder.

If she kept touching me, I was going to spill. I rose, then put her in the center of my bed. Big green eyes looked up at me, dazed with need and hunger.

It only took me seconds to kick my jeans off.

"Show me that pussy, sunflower."

Her chest hitched, and she let her thighs fall open. She was soaked for me, her body trembling.

"Going to take all of me?" I gave my cock a pump.

"Yes." Color filled her cheeks.

"Going to take me hard?"

"Yes, Colt." She writhed on my bed.

It was a picture I would have burned into my brain for the rest of my life.

Quickly, I opened the bedside table drawer and pulled out a condom. I tore the packet open and rolled the latex on.

Then I was on the bed, covering her body with mine. I caught her hair, twisting it in my fist and tilted her head back. I scraped my teeth down her neck, then bit.

She cried out.

I shoved her thighs apart, lining my cock up right where we both wanted it.

Fucking hell. I was holding on by a thread. I nudged the

fat head of my cock right between her folds. She was swollen and slick.

Her hands clenched on my arms. "*Yes.* Come inside me."

"This isn't going to be easy or gentle, Macy."

Her eyes flared. "Good."

With a growl, I drove inside her.

She cried out, the sound garbled.

Fuck, she was tight. "Take me."

"So full." Her teeth sank into her lip. "You're too big."

"You'll take every inch." I pulled out and thrust back inside her warmth. I pushed her thighs up, opening her for me. Then, I started thrusting inside her.

She raked her nails across my shoulders. Need and pleasure twisted through me, and was all tied up with a vicious need to possess.

I felt her pulse around my cock. She was loving it. How rough I was. How much I needed her.

"Like my cock, baby?" My voice was deep and gritty.

"Yes. *Faster*. Oh—"

A second later, she was coming. Fuck me. I held on and watched her. So damn gorgeous. I kept pounding into her. "I want more."

She clung to me, her face flushed. "Take it."

I pulled out, ignoring her cry. On my knees, I twisted her hips over so she was partly on her side. Gripping her waist, I surged back into her. I had more leverage, could fuck her harder and watch her face.

I kept pounding into her, feeling heat building inside me. I wouldn't last much longer. I moved my hand down her belly, lower, then found her clit.

One pinch and another orgasm hit her.

She screamed my name, and I sped up my thrusts. I was so close.

"God, *fuck*." I drove deep, watching her take me. I shuddered as pleasure ripped through me. "*Macy*."

I poured myself inside her. Then, boneless, I dropped to the bed beside her. Rolling, I dragged her with me.

We were both covered in a sheen of perspiration, and the smell of sex lingered. She snuggled into me, making a cute sound.

Tugging her closer, I buried my face in her hair. The sweet weight of her felt good. I wanted to take care of her. Feed her. Run her a bath. Kiss away any aches.

I wanted to protect her. Not just from Warner. From everything—big and small.

My gut hardened. She felt like mine, and it made me scowl at the ceiling.

I'd never wanted to keep a woman before. Never had the desire or patience for it. Never thought I'd be any good at it.

Maybe it was just because I hadn't met Macy.

27

MACY

Usually, I woke up early, ready to take on whatever adventures the day threw at me.

Today, I felt happy to snuggle up to a pillow that smelled like Colt.

Oh.

I cracked an eye open and realized what had woken me. A finger was lazily gliding up and down my spine. I was lying on my stomach, naked, my body with a few interesting aches in interesting places.

"I can tell you're awake."

Mmm, I loved the deep rumble of Colt's sleep-husky voice. Not that we'd gotten much sleep. No, I'd lost track of how many times Colt had slid that big cock of his inside me.

I felt a little twinge of nerves. I wasn't sure how he was going to react.

His finger traced over my shoulder blades, and I shivered. Then it traveled lower, taking his time until he stroked a little between the cheeks of my ass.

"I usually like getting up early," I said.

He made an amused sound. "Why am I not surprised."

"Carpe diem, big guy. You always need to seize the day."

He grunted. "In that case." He gave my ass a firm squeeze.

Taking a deep breath, I rolled over. Then I stilled. His rugged face looked relaxed, and there was a hint of a smile on his lips.

God, that smile. My belly did a strange twist that it only did when Colton Fury smiled.

"I expected you to be all surly, and think this was a mistake."

His smile disappeared, but he cupped my face. "Not a mistake, but I'm still not sure this is good for us. For you."

His words pricked at me. I swallowed. "You don't need to worry. I promised you no strings and no complications." I lifted an arm. "Look, no strings in sight."

His gaze shifted to my breasts.

"Colt?"

"Mmm?" He cupped my breast and thumbed my nipple.

I was wet in an instant, and shifted my legs on the sheets.

His hooded gaze met mine. "We should shower and get dressed."

I smoothed my hands up his bare chest. He had so many hard, interesting muscles. "I have some other ideas."

His lips twitched. "I'd like to see them, but Daisy's due home soon."

I froze. "What?" In a panic, I flew out of bed. I had no desire to get caught naked, with a naked Colt, by that sweet, little girl.

"Don't panic. We have time." He rose, and I saw his muscles flex.

Mmm. My gaze dropped to his hard thighs, and his half-hard cock.

"Macy?"

Jolting, I jerked my gaze up. "Shower!" Whirling, I raced into his bathroom.

It was a darker, moodier version of the guest bathroom, with cool, gray, hexagonal tiles on the floor. I flicked on the water in the shower stall, then after spotting a pink hair tie on the vanity—pretty sure that was Daisy's and not Colt's—I shoved my hair up on top of my head and tied it in a messy bun.

I stepped under the spray. A second later, the shower door opened, and Colt stepped in with me.

I stared at him, watching the water slide over his body. Butterflies took off in my belly. His body was impressive. I watched the water track over his pecs, down his defined abs, lower.

He reached past me and grabbed a bottle of shower gel. He squirted some in his hands and the smell of limes hit me. I knew it.

"I don't have any flowery, girly soap for you. You're going to smell like me."

"I already do." I blushed.

He smoothed his soapy hands down my arms, then back up, and across my shoulders.

I gasped. The long, lazy caresses were drugging. I tipped my head back. Those rough hands slid down my body, then squeezed my ass.

"I love the sounds you make when I touch you," he murmured.

Heat filled me and I squirmed. His hand slid between my legs, and two fingers slid right inside me.

I choked out his name.

"I love when you scream my name, Macy. Especially when you're full of my cock." His mouth took mine. I clutched at him, kissing him back, lost in the pleasure.

"We don't have time," I panted.

"Then I'll have to be quick."

He pulled his hand away, and boosted me up. I quickly wrapped my legs around his hips.

Shower sex always worried me. I was pretty sure it was a quick path to getting a head injury. But Colt's arms felt secure. I trusted him.

"Condom?" I asked.

"Already on."

"I like a man who's well-prepared."

In the next second, my back was against the cool tiles, and his cock was between my legs.

He thrust inside me.

Then I couldn't think of anything but the deluge of hot pleasure, and screaming his name again.

28

COLT

Flipping burger patties on the grill on the deck, I looked back into the living room through the open sliding doors.

There was music blaring. Some pop song that made my ears bleed. My gaze locked on Daisy and Macy.

My daughter held Macy's hands, and the two of them were dancing around like they were possessed. I saw Daisy say something, then wrap her arms around Macy's waist. My woman hugged my little girl back.

My chest squeezed. *Shit.* My hands tightened on the tongs.

When had I started to think of Macy as mine?

Probably from the moment I'd first slid my cock inside her.

No. It had been before that.

I kept watching as Macy and Daisy started dancing again. I could see how much my daughter loved Macy.

For years, I'd shunned the possibility of a relationship to protect my little girl. She'd come first. Always.

And I'd never met a woman I'd wanted to claim.

Wanted to keep.

Now, though, I wanted to keep Macy Underwood.

Throat tight, I watch the pair keep dancing to a new song, giggling wildly.

I cleared my throat. For now, I had to focus on getting Macy safe. That was the most important thing.

"Hey, that salad isn't going to make itself," I called out.

They both spun to face me.

Daisy pulled a face. "I don't want salad."

"You'll eat it, or there'll be no dessert."

She huffed. "But it's so green. It tastes yuck."

"I like salad," Macy said.

My little girl turned. "You do?"

"Yes, as long as it has a yummy dressing on it. Vinaigrette, French, Caesar, ranch—"

"I like ranch," Daisy announced.

"Then we'll have ranch dressing on our salad tonight."

Daisy beamed at Macy, and Macy leaned down and whispered something in her ear. Then Daisy kept dancing as Macy headed my way.

Everything inside me tightened. Since Daisy had returned home this morning, Macy had been careful not to touch me.

Meanwhile, my hands were itching to feel her smooth skin again. She was wearing a short blue skirt and white T-shirt, with dangling hoop earrings.

"It looks like you're pretty good at manning the grill."

"I'm a half-decent cook, but nowhere in Lola's territory."

"No one is in Lola's territory."

Macy was close enough that I could smell my shower gel on her, but it smelled different on her skin. Better.

I couldn't stop myself. I reached out and tugged her to

my side. She startled, and shot a glance toward Daisy. "Colt..."

I rested my chin on the top of her head. "I missed holding you."

I heard her suck in a breath, then she relaxed against me.

This. I wanted this. Not just the hot fucking. The quiet moments, too.

Damn. How had this happened?

My cellphone rang, and the James Bond theme song rang out.

"That's Reath."

Macy stepped back with a laugh. "I like the ring tone. Did he used to be a secret agent?" When I didn't reply, her eyes widened. "Really?"

I pressed the phone to my ear. "Reath?"

"Hey," my brother said. "I found the brownie woman. Her name's Marsha Wade."

My body locked. "Where is she?"

"At my office."

"I'm on my way." I turned the grill off.

"Colt?" Macy's worried eyes met mine.

"Lunch will have to wait. Reath found the woman who came to my office with the brownies."

Macy sucked in a breath.

"I'm going to question her."

Macy straightened. "I'm coming, too."

"No, stay here with Daisy."

"Colt." Her voice was firm, and she grabbed my arm. "This is my life, big guy. I'm coming."

My hands flexed. Damn her for being so stubborn.

"Let me call Lola to take care of Daisy."

After we dropped a sulky Daisy off to Lola, and I'd

endured Daisy's vocal protest about why she should come with us, we headed to PSS.

It was just a few warehouses down from my office, but bigger and slicker than mine. Reath employed a team of people with varied backgrounds.

I took Macy's hand and squeezed it. Then I nodded at the young man at the desk. "Warwick."

He nodded and smiled. "Hi, Colt. Go on up. Reath is waiting for you in the conference room."

I lifted my chin and headed up the stairs. I saw Macy taking it all in.

"This place is shinier than I thought Reath would go for."

She was right. This glossy office was just the front of PSS. Behind the scenes was where the real work happened, and there was far less gloss back there.

Through a glass wall, I saw Reath standing with his arms crossed over his chest.

There was a woman sitting at the long conference table who was fiddling with her big hair and shooting Reath a sulky glare that made me think of Daisy when I told her no.

I opened the door and ushered Macy inside. When the woman looked up, her face changed, and her mouth dropped open. She got what I guessed was a flirty look.

"Oh, Colton. You're even hotter in real life."

Reath made a noise. *Fucker*. I'm glad he was amused.

I'd run into a few women like this before. They saw bounty hunters as celebrities.

"I'm Marsha," she said in a breathy voice.

"Did you work with Scott Warner to hurt Macy?" I growled.

Marsha froze.

"Answer me."

The woman looked at Macy, then gave her a dismissive glance. "I came to see you—"

I strode forward and slammed a fist on the table. Marsha jumped.

"You nearly killed her."

Marsha flinched. "I didn't mean to hurt anyone."

I made a sound, then felt a touch on my arm.

"Colt."

I straightened, and tucked Macy under my arm. I saw Marsha note the move and her shoulders sagged.

"Talk now, or my brothers and I will pick your life apart and make it very uncomfortable for you—at work, where you shop, where you socialize."

The woman swallowed, and toyed with her hair.

"Scott Warner," I said.

"I didn't know his name. He was some sort of fitness junkie. Looked like those guys who preen around in the gym." She sniffed.

Reath stepped forward, and rested a tablet in front of her. There was a photo of Scott Warner on the screen.

Marsha nodded. "That's him. He told me to go to your office, and intimidate her a little."

"He tell you to put coconut in the fucking brownies?" Under my laser glare, she withered.

"He said it would just make her a little sick. I used coconut oil, so it wouldn't be noticed."

A wave of fury hit me. Whatever she saw on my face, it made her blanch.

Macy ran a soothing hand down my arm. "I have a severe allergy to coconut. I had an anaphylactic reaction."

"She nearly died," I growled.

Marsha licked her lips, her face pale. "I'm sorry. I never

wanted to kill anyone. That guy, he said he loves you, and that you won't talk to him. And I love Colt."

"You don't even know me, woman."

She clamped her lips together.

Macy stepped forward. "Scott, my abusive asshole ex, is good at manipulating people."

"Don't you fucking forgive her." Damn, Macy was just too bloody nice.

"She's just a pawn, Colt. Scott used her."

I ran a hand through my hair, then sighed. "Get her out of here."

Reath nodded, then waved to Marsha.

The woman rose, tears in her eyes. "I'm sorry."

Tension vibrated inside me. Then Macy wrapped her arms around me. I breathed her in and relaxed.

"I need to find Warner." He couldn't hide forever. It was time to step things up.

"Let's just go home for now, okay?"

I couldn't say no to her, and even more so, that was exactly where I wanted her. "Okay."

29

MACY

Stirring a pot full of deliciousness on the stove, I took in a lungful of glorious scent.

Lola had made us shrimp and sausage gumbo. My stomach was rumbling.

After talking to Marsha, we'd come back for a late lunch with Daisy. The little girl was now asleep in the main house with Lola. She was starting school tomorrow. I'd read her three stories, Colt had read her two. I smiled. The girl was talented at drawing out bedtime.

Now we were waiting for Dante and Mila to arrive for a late dinner. I stirred the gumbo. I was pretty sure Colt had invited them to try and keep me distracted.

I blew out a breath. Scott really wanted to hurt me. Getting that woman to feed me coconut... It was just crazy.

I was scared, but it was tempered by the fact that Colt was taking care of me. My grump could be pretty sweet. I pulled out some plates. I realized how comfortable I was getting in his place after only a few days. It had been very domestic, hanging out with Daisy, making and eating meals together.

Like a family.

I rubbed my chest. It had always just been mom and me. The two musketeers. But having a bigger group of people to care about...

It didn't feel like the anchor my mom had always said it would be. Holding you back from living life and going places.

Today, I'd liked being with Colt. And Daisy.

And last night... I shivered. Yes, I'd really liked that.

A hard body pressed against my back, and I tilted my head. "Hello."

"Hey." He pushed my hair to one side, and dropped a kiss to my bare shoulder. I'd changed into a maxi dress. I loved the halter top and long skirt. It had a pretty floral pattern of red poppies.

Colt snaked an arm around me, and splayed his hand over my belly. It felt like forever since he'd touched me. His teeth scraped my neck and I gasped.

"I have plans for you later," he murmured.

I gripped his forearms. "Really?"

"Yes. You going to be a good girl for me?"

I spun and met his gaze. "No."

With a groan, he lowered his head. I slid my arms around his neck and kissed him back. Things were just getting interesting when I heard a throat clearing.

I looked up. Dante and Mila were standing there, grinning at us.

"Hi." I smiled, and tried to step away from Colt.

Except he held me tight and wouldn't let me move.

"Something smells great," Mila said.

She looked stylish in a short, navy skirt and a flirty, white blouse.

"We can't take the credit," I said. "It's Lola's work."

"That woman is a miracle." Mila set a bottle of wine down on the island. "We brought a good Pinot."

"That sounds great. I'd love a glass."

"Good, because these two will probably have beer." She jerked a thumb at Dante and Colt.

Soon, I found myself seated beside Colt, listening to Dante talk about his nightclub, bar, and restaurants.

"Mila is busy planning some special events."

"Dante's been having an annual charity gala, but I decided we should have some smaller, more intimate events throughout the year." She smiled. "And make more money for Northstar."

"Northstar?" I asked.

"It's a charity that Dante started." Mila shot a quick look at Colt. "All the Fury brothers support it. It helps kids just out of foster care, with work, accommodation, college."

I turned in my chair. "Really?"

"It's a good charity," Colt said. "A lot of these kids have no one."

Warmth filled my chest. Under the table, I pressed a hand to his thigh. He was such a good guy.

Mila cocked her head. "Dante runs the charity events, but I hear that you're a little more hands on, Colt."

I felt his thigh tense. "Oh?"

Mila smiled. "Yes. The organizers at Northstar told me about one of their programs called FosterBank. Colt started it."

I had no idea what she was talking about.

Colt cleared his throat. "It's nothing."

"Hardly," Mila said. "For many foster families, they can feed a child, but don't always have enough money for the extras. The FosterBank is a place where people can donate clothes, shoes, car seats, school items, and even diapers. Everything a foster family might need for their kids."

I looked at Colt. "You started this?"

He shrugged. "I know some foster families need support. And I saw so many donations not getting where they needed to be. It's really all the people at Northstar."

"That's not what Carmen at Northstar said." Mila sipped her wine. "She says you sometimes stop by and help sort the donations."

A level 2 scowl appeared on his face. "Carmen sure talks a lot."

Smiling, I leaned in and kissed his bearded cheek. "Hot bounty hunter with a heart of gold. Makes you even hotter."

Under the table, he squeezed my knee.

Once dinner was finished, I was feeling warm and happy. Good food, good wine, good company, hot guy who I really wanted to get naked with later.

"Colt, whiskey?" Dante leaned back in his chair. "I brought a bottle of WhistlePig with me. The Boss Hog VII Magellan's Atlantic edition."

"Sounds expensive," Colt said.

"It is. And good. Ladies?"

Mila rose. "I think Macy and I will finish this excellent Pinot. On the terrace." She topped off our wine glasses.

I followed her out onto the rooftop terrace, skirting past Colt's massive grill. It was a balmy New Orleans evening, and the warm breeze ruffled my hair.

"Doing okay?"

I looked at Mila and sipped my wine. "Yes. I've learned to roll with the punches. Pick myself up and dust myself off when I need to."

"And only depend on yourself and never ask for help."

My belly tightened. "That's what my mom taught me. It was only the two of us, until she died of cancer."

"I'm so sorry." Mila leaned against the railing. "I lost my parents. They were killed by the bad guys who were after me."

I sucked in a sharp breath. "Mila, I'm so sorry."

"Thanks. I miss them every day." She paused. "Dante's helped." She rolled her eyes. "He's made me talk to a grief counselor. Being with him, it really helps the most. I tried to go it alone, but having someone to lean on, to hold my hand, to hold me up when everything seems too much..." She turned toward me. "It makes all the difference."

"I promised Colt no strings and no complications." I felt jittery inside, and wiped my hands on my skirt.

"It looks to me like he doesn't mind the strings."

I glanced at him and Dante through the glass door. They were so different, yet it was so easy to tell they were connected, were brothers.

The truth was, I wanted more. I wanted Colt. And I was falling for Daisy, too. I pressed my hand to the base of my neck. But what if I started to need them, and eventually, Colt didn't want me anymore?

My mom always said it was easier to hold on lightly. If you held on too tight, it hurt too much when it was ripped away.

Nothing lasts forever, Macy Moo. Never forget that.

Mila grabbed my shoulder and squeezed. "You're not alone, Macy. Remember that."

30

COLT

Something was wrong with Macy. Again.

Dante and Mila had gone. It had been a good evening. I'd planned it to keep Macy's mind off things, so she didn't worry.

I'm not sure I'd succeeded.

I watched her putting things away in the kitchen. Her brow was creased, there was no humming, no smile.

My hands clenched. I didn't want her to be worried and scared. When I walked into the kitchen, she didn't even hear me.

"Macy?"

She jerked. "Oh, Colt. I'm nearly done here."

I took the wine glass she was drying from her hand and set it on the counter. "What's wrong?"

She glanced away. "Nothing. It was a great night. Mila and Dante are wonderful."

I wasn't very good with words. Lord knew if I could avoid talking with people, I would. I didn't know what to say to make her feel better.

I'd always been more of a man of action. So instead, I

pulled her against my chest, and when she didn't fight me, a bit of the pressure in my gut eased.

I might not have the words, but I could show Macy that she was safe.

Show her that she was mine.

"Come on." I took her hand and led her to the stairs.

She frowned. "Where are we going?"

"Somewhere you'll like."

Instead of heading down to the bedroom level, I took her up. There was a door at the top and I entered the code into the lock.

When we walked out onto the rooftop of my warehouse, the warm evening wrapped around us. Lights clicked on and Macy gasped.

"Colt. Oh, wow."

I watched her face as she took in the pool. There were some potted plants that Lola kept alive, and comfy, wide loungers. The pool glowed blue, and beyond it, was a great view of New Orleans.

"It's a perfect little paradise." She shot me a smile.

That smile was like a punch to my sternum. There. Finally, a smile. "Want to swim?"

Her eyes widened. "I don't have a swimsuit."

"So?" I sat on the end of a pool lounger.

Macy licked her lips and scanned around.

Sure enough, that free spirit of hers took over. She untied the top of her dress. It slithered down her body and pooled at her feet. She stood there in just her underwear and in an instant, my cock was rock hard.

So beautiful. I took in the slim limbs, the golden skin. She shot me a flirty look, then took her time discarding her bra and panties.

She walked into the water, giving me a perfect view of her peach of an ass.

Fuck. Just watching her and I was ready to blow. She swam a few laps, her sexy body on display for me in the water.

Then her head broke the surface, and she stared up at me. "Are you coming in, Mr. Fury?"

I rose and yanked my shirt off. My jeans and boxer shorts were next. I felt her hungry gaze on me as I walked to the steps.

Yes, I could show Macy just how much I wanted her.

And that she was mine.

The water wasn't cold. I waded in and strode straight to her.

She leaped straight into my arms, wrapping her arms and legs around me.

"You know, a lot of people are intimidated by me."

She snorted. "You mean scared of your grumpiness."

"You never have been."

The muted light of the pool danced over her features, making her look like a fairy. "Because I know you're all bark, and very little bite."

I growled, and put my mouth on her neck. I bit her and she laughed, writhing against me.

"There are lots of people who would disagree. From day one you never cowered."

She arched a brow. "I'm guessing all your other office managers cowered."

"Office *assistants*. And yes, they did, and then they all quit."

She cupped my cheeks. "It was two days after I started, I saw you with Daisy. Even though you were driving me crazy, I saw that you were a good dad, and I knew. Grumpy exterior and gooey interior."

I kissed her.

I pulled her as close as I could, drawing in the taste of her.

Eventually, she wiggled free, panting. Even in the shadows, I saw the desire on her face. She pushed me back toward the steps.

"Sit," she ordered. "On the top step."

I obeyed. The top step put most of my body out of the water, and the air was cool on my wet skin. My hard cock was also rising out of the water.

Macy pressed her hands to my thighs, then knelt on the step below.

Fuck. My gut was hard as iron. My very wet, very sexy woman was kneeling between my legs. Her warm hand wrapped around my swollen cock.

"Macy."

"I love when your voice gets extra growly like that."

I couldn't take my eyes off her. She leaned forward and pressed her mouth to the head of my cock.

My body locked, every muscle tight. I felt like she was pulling things out from deep inside me. Breaking open things that I'd always kept locked up.

I slid a hand into her wet hair. "What do you want, my wild, sexy sunflower?"

"You."

"My cock?"

She nodded.

My hands tightened in her hair and her lips parted. "Say it."

"I want your cock. In my mouth."

I hissed. "Suck it." My voice was little more than gravel.

Macy moaned, then sucked me deep, taking half my cock in her hot mouth.

I couldn't breathe, but I didn't give a shit. All I could do was watch this woman—my woman—worship my cock. My fingers tightened in her hair. She sucked harder, her head bobbing.

My groan was loud. The sounds she was making said she was loving it.

I was loving it.

She swayed in the water, drawing my gaze to her bare ass. She kept working my cock, drawing groans from me. Electricity arced through my body. She went deeper and gagged. Gently, I massaged her skull, finding it sexy that she was choking on my cock, but still had a determined glint in her eyes.

I flexed my ass, watched her eyelids flutter. My lower back was tight, pleasure heavy in my gut. Her mouth was hot, tight, and wet.

But I didn't want to come down Macy's throat. I wanted her with me. I didn't want to come alone. I wanted us together.

Pulling her off me, I slid my hands under her arms and lifted her. I carried her out of the water and to one of the pool loungers. Then I laid her on it.

Damn. Macy's sweet body, wet and flushed, and all mine. Her gaze was locked on me.

Then I remembered. "Fuck, I don't have a condom up here."

"Well... I don't mind, if you don't. I mean, I've had a physical since I left California. You have a copy of it in my employment records. And I'm on the Pill."

My brain stopped functioning. *Take her bare?*

I was suddenly overcome with the need to make Macy

mine. She already felt like mine.

I wanted to mark her.

"I'm clean."

"Good." Her chest rose and fell quickly.

I shoved her legs wide and she gasped. I gripped my cock, lining up, then I thrust home.

Our moans mingled. Her hands gripped me, her nails biting into my skin.

"*Colt*."

I slid in and out, finding a hard, fast rhythm. Flesh slapped against flesh. Leaning over her, I sank my teeth into her neck. Her sexy cry was perfect. She strained against me, silently demanding more.

Demanding everything.

I pumped faster. I wouldn't last much longer with this sweet pussy gripping my cock. I could tell she was getting close. I moved my hand, and stroked where we were connected. Where she was stretched around me. Then I found her swollen clit, and after one rub, she screamed.

Fuck. I loved that sound.

Her body was shaking, and I couldn't hold back. My climax hit hard, slamming into me. On a long groan, I leaned back and pulled out of her.

With a firm grip on my cock, I jerked, shooting across her belly.

She gasped, and I was nearly blind from the intense pleasure rocketing through me. I watched my come mark her skin, and satisfaction hit me. I kept coming, ribbons of white striping her.

Then when I was done, I fell forward and caught myself on my fists.

Green eyes met mine. Her face was soft, her fingers

moving. My gut clenched. She was running them over her belly, through my come.

"I like your pool."

I barked out a laugh. "I'm glad." I paused, feelings I couldn't name swirling inside me. "Macy..." Shit, once again, I didn't have any words.

She smiled. "I know." She lifted her head and kissed me.

I nipped her bottom lip. "How about I reacquaint you with my shower and bed?"

Her smile widened. "Okay." Then her gaze dropped, tracing down my body to my already hardening cock. "Maybe some other things, too."

31

MACY

"I need to change my hair," Daisy wailed.

The little girl was all dressed—in cute shorts, and a white shirt with a rainbow on the front. Her glossy, brown hair was in a slightly crooked ponytail that Colt had just finished.

I saw him sigh. "It's fine."

"No, Daddy. It's *wrong*."

"You're going to be late for school."

I headed over, and Lola gave me a wink.

We'd just eaten breakfast in the main house. I loved the way the sunlight filled the space, and there was a vase of fresh lilies on the island that had to be Lola's handiwork. I loved Colt's warehouse too—it was more masculine and moody. A space that I knew was his haven. Where he could be himself.

I reached Daisy and quickly straightened her ponytail, then pulled out the pink ribbon from my own hair.

"Look." I showed it to her, then tied it in her hair.

She raced to the nearby mirror, arching in a way only kids or contortionists could manage. "It's pretty."

"Like you. And I have something else." I held up the origami flower I'd made her.

"A sunflower." Daisy took it.

"For luck." It was bright yellow with some orange folded into the center. "First day back at school used to always make me nervous."

Daisy blew out a breath. "I'm sad the summer is over."

I nodded. "I get that. The best thing about summer is that it comes around again."

She perked up.

"And there are other things to look forward to," I continued. "The Fall, Halloween, Christmas—"

"And my birthday!"

I ruffled her hair. "Exactly. You need to focus on the positive stuff."

Her nose wrinkled. "Daddy says to always have a contingency plan."

I snorted. That sounded exactly like Colt. I flicked a glance at him. He was watching us, a strange look on his face that I couldn't read.

"Well, that can't hurt when you're a bounty hunter. Are you a bounty hunter?"

Daisy giggled. "No."

"Then maybe worry about contingency plans when you're older."

"Time to go," Lola said. "We don't want to be late."

Daisy threw her arms around my waist and my heart melted. I hugged her and patted her back. "Have an awesome day, gorgeous girl."

"I will." She raced to Colt, who scooped her up.

"Love you, short stuff."

"Love you, Daddy."

Oh, God. It hit me in the solar plexus. That pure love. I turned to the side, trying to get a grip on my emotions.

Lola, who was watching me, smiled. Then she and Daisy hurried out.

I turned to Colt. He looked his usual hot, grumpy self. His jeans hugged his fine ass. Now that we were alone, my thoughts turned very X-rated. My lower belly clenched tight, and instantly I was back by the pool. Feeling him inside me, then coming on me.

After the pool last night, he'd fucked me again in his bed. It had been slower, lazier, but just as hot. And his gaze had been locked on mine as he'd moved inside me. Like he was memorizing every second.

"Macy?"

I jerked. "Sorry, I'm..."

"Daydreaming."

"Maybe."

A slow smile crossed his face. "I think I can guess the topic of your daydream."

My skin flushed hot, my breasts felt full. How did he do this to me? I lifted my chin. "We need to get to the office."

He sighed. "We do. I'm going to find Warner today. I'm going to end this."

Then I wouldn't be in danger. I wouldn't need to stay here anymore. It would be safe to go back to my place.

Before I could process that, Colt's cellphone rang. He pulled it out.

"Fury." His frown deepened. "Okay." He waved a hand at me. "Turn on the TV. The news."

I hurried over and grabbed the remote. The TV flickered to life.

"Breaking news," a glossy, female reporter said, her face

serious. "Notorious rapist Wayne Cullen has escaped from prison—"

I gasped, watching the report. Cullen had cut a trail of terror for single women across most of the South before he'd been caught in New Orleans a few months back. Behind me, I heard the low murmur of Colt's voice as he talked to whoever was on the phone.

I wrapped my arms around my middle, listening to the long list of victims left by this animal. And he'd gotten free and attacked several young women in a sorority house early this morning.

God. It put my own troubles in perspective. Those poor girls.

"Yeah. Let me call you back."

I tore my gaze off the TV and looked at Colt. His face was so hard and grim.

"Wayne Cullen escaped."

"I saw." I clenched my hands together. "He attacked some girls at a sorority house."

A muscle ticked in Colt's jaw. "Yeah. It hasn't been released yet, but he raped three young women. He beat one of them to death, and put another one in a coma."

"Oh, God." Nausea hit me. "They want you to find him?"

One brisk nod.

"Go."

"I don't want to leave you. Warner—"

I waved a hand. "This is more important."

He took a step closer. "Not to me."

Now my insides were a gooey, sticky mess. "I'll stay at the office. With one of Reath's men."

Colt hesitated.

"This is really important, Colt." I stabbed a finger at the TV. "You have to stop Cullen before he hurts anyone else."

Colt closed the distance between us and gripped my shoulders. "You'll stay in the office."

"Yes."

"You won't go anywhere alone—"

"I promise." I went up on my toes and kissed his jaw. "I'll be here waiting for you. However long it takes."

He kissed me, his tongue stealing into my mouth. I held on tight.

"I'll find this asshole, then I'll find the asshole who's after you."

32

MACY

"Wow, I figured I'd get one of your security guards, not you."

I made sure the front door of Colt's warehouse was locked, then turned.

Reath smiled, which I took two seconds to appreciate. Damn, the man was fine.

"I was free."

We fell into step.

"And if something happened to you, my brother would lose his mind."

I missed a step, then caught myself. "We're...it's not..." I blew out a breath. "It's casual. We're just enjoying ourselves."

Reath's face didn't change. "You don't really believe that."

"I promised him no complications, and that I'd keep my strings to myself."

Reath didn't say a word, but I felt the weight of his gaze. Suddenly I felt like squirming, baring my soul.

Words spilled out of me. "I don't usually do strings anyway. I like to keep things free, easy, fun."

"Mmm."

"God, you don't say anything, and I feel like you're pulling out my deepest secrets." I frowned. "How do you do that?"

"It's my superpower."

I made a harrumphing sound. "Were you really a spy?"

"If I tell you, then I'd have to kill you." He grabbed my arm. We stopped on the corner by Smokehouse, Dante's bar.

"Macy, I'm no expert on relationships." He was talking to me, but I saw him scanning the street. Something told me he'd clocked every car, every person, and probably memorized every license plate. "But I think you and Colt need to stop saying the things you usually do, and actually share how you feel."

Big emotions welled inside me like a balloon. I knew exactly what it was I was feeling. Fear.

I cleared my throat. "Right now, he doesn't need anything distracting him from catching the bad guy. Bad *guys*, if you count both Cullen and Scott."

We started walking again.

I unlocked the office and headed for my desk. I stashed my handbag in the drawer. I had to admit, the short commute to work rocked.

Reath disappeared into Colt's office and I heard a cellphone ring. When I heard a low murmur, I knew he was on the phone.

I got to work and checked my email first. I deleted all the spam. Ugh, I swear the spam emails multiplied. Didn't people have better things to do with their time than send spam? I wondered how Colt was doing. Wayne Cullen targeted women, but he was dangerous to everyone.

Colt will be fine.

There was an email from an unfamiliar sender called ForYou99. The subject said For Macy. Frowning, I opened it.

Then my body froze, and the tang of bile filled my mouth.

There were photos...of me. But not of me. The horrible pictures showed a woman tied up, handcuffed, bloody. Her body was naked, and my head had been photoshopped onto her.

My stomach whirled sickeningly, and for a second, I worried I'd need the trashcan under my desk so I could be sick.

I took a deep breath. In for four, hold, and out for four. I did it again, and the urge to hurl passed. I made myself look at the pictures again.

There was some text as well.

You're mine, Macy. We'll have so much fun. Just like we used to.

Despair welled. Why was he doing this? I pressed my hands flat to the desk. I knew this wasn't my fault, that it was all on Scott.

My first instinct was to tell Colt. But he needed to stay focused. Scott wanted us upset and off-balance.

I could tell Reath, but I knew he'd tell Colt. Colt would lose his mind.

Straightening in my chair, I clicked delete.

"Okay?"

I managed, by the smallest amount, not to jolt. I glanced up at Reath in the doorway. I couldn't show any reaction, or he'd know. The way he was watching me, I guessed he already knew something.

"I'm fine." I pasted on a smile. "The usual spam to give my delete finger a workout." I wiggled my pointer finger. "You want some coffee? I'll put on a pot."

"Sure."

I tugged on my ear. "When do you think we'll hear from Colt?"

"When he has time to call. He'll be busy for a bit."

I nodded, fiddling with my hair.

"He's good at his job, Macy. He'll be fine."

"I know."

"In the meantime, I'll work on finding Warner."

"Thanks. I know this is all so much trouble."

Without making a sound, Reath appeared right at the edge of my desk. The man really could move quietly.

"It's no trouble at all. Get that out of your head. My brothers and I protect what's ours. That includes you."

I pressed a hand to my churning belly. "I'm not used to having someone look out for me."

He leaned down. "Get used to it."

"How can I ever repay you all? Repay Colt?"

"We don't want payment, Macy. We want you safe." He paused. "If you want to do something for Colt, just be there for him when he gets back. These jobs, they're never easy. It takes a toll."

I frowned. "He's always seemed fine in the past."

"He usually takes a night before he comes home. Shakes it off."

Alone. Not wanting to bring the darkness back to Daisy, to his family.

Reath wasn't finished. "He loves to blame himself, for not being quicker, smarter—"

I jerked to my feet. "That's crazy. It's *not* his fault."

Reath watched me for a beat. "That urge to blame himself runs deep in Colt."

From long ago. I clutched my hands together. From losing his mom, his sister.

Reath nodded, like he could hear my thoughts. "Be there for him, Macy."

33

COLT

Swinging out of my truck, I slammed the door.

It didn't help.

Frustration, anger, and tiredness were a bad combination.

I waved to Reath's guard on the way into my garage. At least Reath had kept me updated, and I knew everyone was safe.

Cullen was still on the loose. I scowled. I'd tracked him to an abandoned house where he'd holed up, but the guy was as slippery as a... I was too tired to think of a decent fucking simile. Hell, I only knew what a simile was because Daisy had been learning about them a few months back.

Cullen had run. I'd chased him across several backyards before I'd lost him. I blew out a breath, and headed upstairs.

Reath had left a message, and was following up some leads on Warner. I'd missed seeing Daisy, and finding out how her first day of school had gone. My jaw creaked from grinding my teeth. My little girl would be sleeping soundly now.

Wasn't the first time I'd missed something important, and probably wouldn't be the last. Luckily, she had Lola and my brothers to plug the gaps. And Macy.

Macy had texted me a picture of the two of them at dinner time, both of them with their hair in pigtails and pulling funny faces. I'd saved it as the background on my phone.

It was after 10 PM, so I figured Macy would be asleep, as well. Reath told me she'd had an uninteresting day at the office.

I was in a filthy mood. Deciding I needed a drink to shake things off before I headed upstairs, I exited my warehouse. Dante's nightclub was just across the parking lot his staff used.

When I headed into Ember, I paid little attention to the fancy black and gold décor. The place was full, as it was most nights. I skirted the crowd and found an empty stool at the bar. I nodded at Dante's head bartender, Venus. The attractive Black woman eyed me for a second, then pulled a bottle of bourbon off the top shelf.

"Rough day, Colt?"

"Something like that." She handed me a glass. "Thanks." I took a sip, willing it to wash away the bad taste in my mouth.

Two women in short skirts, laughing and talking, moved up beside me. When they tried to get my attention, I didn't glance their way. I wasn't interested in any company. I stared at the amber fluid in my glass. I rarely drank more than one or two, because it never held any answers, and I never wanted to turn into my father.

The women beside me suddenly fell quiet, and I sensed them looking into the crowd.

"Oh, dibs," one drawled. "He's not from around here, but I want him."

I lifted my head, and saw Boone Hendrix walking toward the bar.

It was clear that he wasn't part of the usual party crowd, and his military training was obvious in the way he moved. He wore dark pants and a gray button-down shirt. He was tall, with broad shoulders and brown hair.

He didn't give the women a single look as he sat on the stool beside me. "Colt."

"Boone. Buy you a drink?"

He eyed my glass. "What are you having?"

"Bourbon. Dante only stocks the good stuff."

"Sure."

I waved at Venus for another bourbon.

"Dante called me," Boone said. "Told me to meet him here." He glanced around. "Fancy."

I lifted my chin. "Norcross said you had a personal protection job down this way."

"Yeah. A guy from Shreveport who'd been getting a few threats. Job was uneventful."

"The best kind. How's Vermont?"

"Good."

"Atlas?"

"Fine. Except my dog will be pissed that I left him with our grizzled, old neighbor. Rex doesn't spoil him like I do." Boone glanced at me. "Heard you're hunting Wayne Cullen."

"Yeah." I tossed back more of my drink. "He got away from me today."

"You'll catch him."

"Just worried it won't be before he hurts another woman."

"That's not on you, Colt."

I looked at Boone. "I could probably say the same to you about a bunch of shit that you're dragging around from your time in the military." Boone had been under Vander's command as part of Ghost Ops. The best of the best of the military's special forces, sent to do the worst jobs in the worst places.

Boone swirled then sipped his drink. "Yeah. And like you, I know it doesn't always help."

We drank together in silence, and finally I pushed my empty glass across the bar. "I'd like to stay, but I need to go. I'm sure Dante will be down here to catch up with you soon."

Boone nodded. "You have a daughter to get back to."

I cleared my throat. "And a woman."

Boone's eyebrows went up. "You? A woman? I knew Dante had taken the fall, but not you."

"We're still...working things out. She has an ex who doesn't want to be an ex."

The other man's face hardened. "If I can help you out with that, let me know. For some reason, Vander's put me up in a hotel for a few days before I fly home." He scowled into his drink.

Vander Norcross was forcing Boone to spend some time in the city and socialize.

"Thanks, Boone." As I rose, I saw Dante coming our way and waved. I didn't stay to talk to Dante. He'd see I was tired, frustrated, and pissed.

It only took me a few minutes to get from Ember back to home. I let myself in and headed up the stairs.

When I stalked into the kitchen, I paused. A floor lamp was on low, as was the light above the stove. They cast a warm, homey glow around the place. I was used to coming home to darkness. Occasionally, one of my brothers might leave a bottle of bourbon for me.

I dropped my keys on the island.

"You're home."

Macy's voice made me spin. I spotted her now, tucked up on my couch. There was an open book discarded beside her, and the red throw blanket that Lola had made me was tucked around her body.

A fist squeezed in my chest, then released. I felt some of the day's shit leak away from me. "You should be in bed."

She rose and tossed the blanket. My gut contracted. She was wearing one of my white T-shirts. It swamped her, and slid off one shoulder.

She looked sexier than anything I'd ever seen.

"I was waiting for you."

Waiting for me? My brain was still trying to compute that, when she wrapped her arms around me.

I hugged her close, and breathed in her scent. Berries—fresh and clean.

"You didn't find him yet?"

I sighed. "I got close, but he slipped away."

She squeezed tighter. "You'll get him tomorrow."

I just fucking prayed he didn't hurt anyone else before I did.

"Hungry?" She pulled back. "I made you some meatloaf. I know it's not super gourmet, but I put my special spices in it. It's really tasty. I wanted to make something that would keep for whatever time you got home."

She'd cooked for me? My throat was tight. "I like meatloaf."

She smiled at me like I'd said I could solve global warming in an instant. "Sit. I'll serve it up."

Before long, I found myself sitting at the island, eating good meatloaf, while Macy updated me on Daisy's day.

This was...nice. I liked it.

"Reath said he hasn't found Scott yet."

Guilt that I wasn't out there looking for the asshole hit me. I grunted. "We're used to faster results, but since Scott isn't local, it's making it easier for him to hide. Plus, he isn't using a credit card, or at least, not one in his name."

Macy huffed out a breath. "Enough about bad guys. You need to switch it off for a bit."

She got off her stool and stepped behind me. She pressed a kiss to the back of my neck, then started kneading my shoulders.

I bit back a moan. It felt so good.

"Relax now, Colt."

"I don't relax."

"You do tonight." She held out a hand, and I took it without hesitating. It was so small and delicate compared to mine. Really, I had no right to be touching it. Touching her.

But in the low light, she smiled at me, that mass of curls framing her face. "Come on." She tugged me, leading me to the stairs.

"Where are we going?"

"Well, my plan is to get you naked."

My cock stirred. It didn't take much with Macy.

She looked back at me over her shoulder, a feminine smile on her face.

It had desire filling me.

"You're going to lie on that big bed of yours, then I'm going to ride that big cock of yours. Sound good?"

I swallowed. "Yeah."

"Good. I'm going to ride you hard, Colt, until you can't

think of anything but me." Her smile faded to a serious look. "I'm going to take care of you."

That wasn't how things worked. I took care of people.

But when we reached the bedroom, and Macy pulled that T-shirt off so that she was naked, I stopped thinking. All there was at that moment was Macy.

34

MACY

I finished braiding Daisy's hair. "What do you think?"

The little girl peered into the mirror, turning her head from side to side. "It's good."

The lackluster tone of her voice matched her face. Colt had stayed long enough this morning to give Daisy a morning hug before he'd headed out again.

I rested my hands on her shoulders and squeezed. "It's hard when your dad's away."

Daisy bit her lip and nodded.

"He does important work," I told her.

She nodded again. "He helps catch bad people."

"Yes. And keeps good people safe."

Daisy looked down at her white and pink shoes. "I know, but..."

I toyed with the end of her braid. "But what, sweetheart?"

She looked up. "What if he doesn't come home? What if he dies? Like my mom did."

"Oh, baby." I hugged her. She smelled like apple shampoo. "I know your daddy will do everything he can to ensure he comes home to you. You're the most important thing in his world."

She rubbed her cheek on my shirt. "You promise?"

"Yes. And remember what I told you? There is no point focusing on the bad stuff. It's better to focus on the good. Think of your daddy catching the bad man and being home for dinner. Maybe not tonight, but as soon as he can."

Daisy nodded and shot me a tremulous smile.

I cupped her cheek. "How about we do something fun tonight? Maybe play some games. Whatever game you want."

Daisy's smile widened. "Poker."

My eyes bugged out of my head. "You can play poker?"

She nodded. "Uncle Kav taught me. We bet using pretzels."

I guessed I shouldn't be surprised; this little girl was being raised by the Fury brothers, after all.

"How about we start with Snap, and go from there?"

She beamed at me. "Okay." She threw her arms around me, hugging me tight. "I'm glad you're here, Macy. I hope you don't go away."

I hugged her back, my throat tight.

Then I waved her and Lola off. Alone, my thoughts turned to Colt.

I bit my lip. *Stay safe, big guy.*

Somehow Colt and his daughter were becoming the center of my universe. I wondered if my mom had been wrong. Colton and Daisy, what I felt for them, seemed like the biggest and best adventure. They made me feel safe, happy. They felt like home. I didn't feel like I was trapped or missing out.

I cleaned the kitchen, and then met my security guard for the walk to the office. As we walked down the sidewalk,

I plucked at my cute, red capri pants. They were a pop of color that I loved. I'd topped them with a simple black shirt.

In the office, I turned on the radio and headed for my desk. Thankfully, there were no horrid emails with ugly pictures from Scott today. I didn't make the assumption that he'd given up. No, he was out there, biding his time.

I popped up a news website on my computer. There were a few articles about Wayne Cullen and a photo of Colt, along with talk about him joining the hunt for the fugitive. He looked so good in the photo, mid-stride, scowl on his face. A man who knew what he was doing and would see it through to the end.

The morning was a blur of filing, phone calls, and invoices. I'd just finished eating a turkey sandwich for lunch, when a breaking news bulletin flashed across my computer screen.

Escaped rapist caught.

My heart hit my ribs so hard it hurt. I tapped the keyboard, just as a report came on.

"Infamous and violent rapist, Wayne Cullen, has finally been caught by well-known, local bounty hunter, Colton Fury."

My smile was huge. Colt had done it. He'd captured Cullen.

Video footage flashed on screen of Colt stalking out of a building. He ignored the cameras. My belly flip-flopped. He looked so hot. A breeze ruffled his hair, and he had a scowl in place. Not to mention that walk of his.

All mine.

The reporter came back on. "Unfortunately, it took another attack for authorities to catch Cullen."

Oh, no. As the reporter detailed how Cullen had broken into a woman's home, I pressed a hand to my chest.

A part of Colt would blame himself for not being fast enough.

"Thankfully, Colton Fury interrupted the attack. The victim is alive and in the hospital in a stable condition. And today, the city of New Orleans will breathe a sigh of relief that Wayne Cullen is once again behind bars. The New Orleans PD are working extra hard to ensure he stays there."

I closed the website. I was so proud of Colt. I needed to make sure he understood that. He'd done the entire city a favor.

And now he'd come back and get to work finding Scott.

I glanced out the window. Cars and people passed by.

Where are you, Scott? I wanted the shadow of him hanging over me gone.

My heart squeezed. I wanted a life with Colt.

Oh boy. I pressed my palm to my belly where it turned over with fear and excitement.

Maybe my mom had been wrong. Maybe I could have more. Maybe I could find my forever.

35

COLT

As I exited New Orleans police headquarters, I saw all the news vans and scowled.

Damn vultures.

They love to pick over the carcass of a situation. Glorify all the gory details, traumatize all the victims again, all in the name of the public deserving the truth.

And I'd be made out to be a fucking hero.

I stomped toward my SUV. I felt a big dose of relief and satisfaction that Cullen was back behind bars. No more young women would be violated or killed.

But Kristen Miller wouldn't think I was a hero. I'd saved her life, but Cullen had already had her for hours.

I rubbed the back of my neck, trying to get a lock on my emotions.

Maybe I should try and follow Macy's advice, and focus on the positive. The job was over. I could get home to my girls.

Shit. I stopped just a few feet from my truck. My girls. Daisy and Macy. I liked that. I wanted that.

Permanently.

I'd get Macy safe from Warner, then I'd convince her to stay. That even when I annoyed and pissed her off, I could make her happy.

My chest ached. Damn, was this what love felt like? Kind of like heartburn?

I knew the love of family—I felt that for my brothers. And I knew the protective love of a parent. I'd die for Daisy.

But what I felt for Macy was mixed up with desire, need, and...fuck, vulnerability.

I didn't do vulnerability well. Usually, I did everything I could *not* to feel vulnerable.

When I reached my SUV, I saw paper fluttering under the wiper blade.

Damn. I scanned around. There was no one nearby. I hoped to hell it was fan mail, but I guessed it wasn't. This had Warner all over it.

I pulled it free. It was a printout of photos and when I saw the content, my gut locked. Anger gripped my throat like a clawed hand.

They were ugly, fucked-up pictures of a woman tied up and splattered with blood.

Macy.

No. I breathed through my nose, my chest heaving. It wasn't Macy. I could tell at a glance that her head had been photoshopped in. Badly.

Fucking Warner.

The paper scrunched in my hand. He was messing with us. Trying to provoke a reaction. I wanted to say I was above giving him one, but these were sick.

I flipped the paper over. When I read the writing, anger slid through my veins.

I have her.

I want what's mine.

Always mine.

Macy. *Fuck.* My pulse took off. I yanked my phone out as I leaped into my SUV. The bastard had Macy.

I dialed her phone. It rang and rang.

"*Fuck.*" I called Reath as I started the engine.

"Colt. I saw you got Cullen. Well done."

"Reath, Warner left me a note. He has Macy." I sped down the street.

"What? No."

"Call your guard."

"I'm doing it now. Brother, I have camera feed of her right now. She's at her desk on a phone call."

I felt sick. "Could your feed have been hacked?"

If Warner hurt her, I'd kill him. I had the means to dispose of a body. No one would ever find him.

"My system can't be hacked. Colt, I have the guard right here on the other line. She's fine. She's at your office with him and perfectly safe."

My hands clenched on the steering wheel. "You're sure?"

"Colt, I'm sure."

I blew out a noisy breath. If Reath was sure, then Macy was fine. "Fuck me. Warner printed out some fucked-up images with Macy's face on them, left them on my truck. He's messing with me."

Reath cursed. "He's watching you. And he knows the best way to mess with your head."

"Okay, I'm almost back to the office." I needed to check with my own two eyes that Macy was okay.

I needed to feel her, touch her, in order for that part of me to settle.

"I'm done waiting for this asshole to slip up. We need to find him. I want him neutralized."

"We'll find him," Reath said.

I parked by the office. As I neared, I saw Macy through the window. She was sitting on top of her desk, folding paper. She was smiling.

Finally, I felt that panicked part of me settle. I pushed open the door.

Her smile got impossibly wider, and she leaped off her desk. "You're back. You caught him."

I scooped her up and slammed my mouth down on hers. She made a sound, then dropped the paper in her hands and threw her arms around my neck. I set her on the desk and devoured her. I couldn't get close enough. I wrapped a hand around her throat, my fingers on the drum of her pulse.

When I lifted my head, she was panting.

"Wow." She licked her lips. "Give me a second for my brain to start working again."

I smiled and cupped her jaw. She was like a ray of sunshine. I saw Reath's guard in the doorway, and nodded at the man. He gave me a chin lift and slipped out quietly.

"I'm so proud of you, big guy."

Her words arrowed into me. "Another woman got hurt."

Macy gripped my arms. "She's alive because of you. And Cullen can't hurt anyone else. You're a hero."

I winced. A label I didn't want. "I'm just glad you're okay."

Macy cocked her head. "You were worried I wasn't?"

I nodded. "Warner left a note on my Suburban."

"Ugh." She dropped her head against my chest.

I decided not to mention the pictures. "He said he had you. And that you were his."

Her eyes sparked. "Well, he doesn't have me, and I'm not, and never will be, his."

"I know." My fingers tightened on her jaw. "Because you're mine."

"Colt," she whispered.

The front door flung open. Lola, gray hair askew and face panicked, rushed in.

I straightened. "Lola?"

"I can't find Daisy. She wasn't at school when I went to get her. I've searched everywhere, Colton." There was fear in the woman's voice. "She's gone."

"No." All the color drained from Macy's face. "No."

The world spun around me, and I felt bombarded by sound and light.

Then I sucked it all in and locked it down.

Scott Warner had my daughter.

That monster had my little girl.

"Colt?" Macy gripped my arm.

But my vision tunneled. All I could think about was Daisy.

"Warner has Daisy."

36

MACY

I followed behind Colt on the way back to his warehouse. He was moving too quickly for me to keep up, even at a jog.

My belly turned in sickening circles.

It didn't seem possible that Scott had taken Daisy. I felt trapped in a nightmare. She was just an innocent, little girl. Nausea welled and I battled it down.

We dropped Lola back at the main house. The worried woman was calling around to the parents of Daisy's friends to see if Daisy was with any of them, or if their children knew where she was.

The Fury brothers were all meeting at Colt's. When we reached the door, Beauden was waiting. His rugged face was grimmer than usual.

"Daisy's missing?" Beau growled.

Colt gave one quick nod. "Inside. The others are on the way."

All the men had dropped everything as soon as Colt had called. Beau shot me a glance, but Colt didn't even look my way.

Guilt wrapped around me, tighter and tighter.

This was my fault. Scott was after me, and I'd brought him into the Fury brothers' lives.

In the living area, Colt paced back and forth, his hands fisted by his side. "Warner has her. I know it."

"Let's get the facts first, then we'll find her," Beau said.

"If he hurts her..."

There was so much torment in Colt's voice. God, Daisy had already lost so much in her short life. So had Colt.

If she didn't come home...

I whirled and ran for the powder room. I slammed the door closed, just as my stomach heaved. I sank down beside the toilet and brought up everything in my stomach.

My skin was hot, my insides were cold.

My fault. All my fault.

We had to bring Daisy home.

When I reemerged, the rest of the Fury brothers had arrived. Dante, clearly recently out of bed, was drinking coffee, his hair tousled. Kavner was in a suit. Reath stood by the island, hip hitched against the stone.

"Warner left this note on my truck. I thought he had Macy, but he meant Daisy." Colt dropped the paper onto the island. Then he snatched up an empty glass and threw it. It smashed against the wall.

Insides roiling, I sat on the couch. No one paid me any attention.

"My guys are pulling CCTV around the school," Reath said.

I curled my legs up. I was so cold. I prayed that Daisy was okay. I hated feeling this useless.

Colt's cellphone rang and he answered it in a flash. "Lola? Okay." He closed his eyes. "Got it. Yeah, I'll find her and bring her home."

When he opened his eyes, they were empty. Like he'd shut down.

"One of Daisy's friends said she saw a man take Daisy. She was fighting him."

"Fuck," Dante said.

Reath opened a laptop. "My team has footage."

The men crowded around the screen.

"It's not a good angle," Kav said.

"That's Warner. Fuck." Colt spun, his hands pressed to the back of his neck. His jaw was locked.

I wanted to soothe him. If not take away his pain, at least share it.

I rose and walked over. "Colt?" I touched his arm.

He didn't pull away, but he didn't come any closer. His body was tense under my fingers.

"I'm sorry," I whispered. "So sorry."

"I should have considered this." His stare was blank, like he didn't even see me. "I should've had security on her."

"I didn't believe Scott was capable of this."

A muscle ticked in Colt's jaw. "The asshole you dated is dangerous. To everyone."

I let my hand drop. I felt about an inch high. Colt was right. I should've seen it. How could I not have seen it?

The men talked, strategizing. It flowed past me, and I felt shut out.

Reath was talking about possible locations Scott could be using. His team was searching traffic cams around the school.

I moved back to the couch, and tried to hold it together. I wished there was something I could do.

The couch moved, and I woodenly looked up.

Kavner was watching me with a sympathetic gaze. "How are you holding up?"

"It's not me who matters, it's Daisy." I glanced over at Colt. He hadn't once looked my way. It was like he'd forgotten I existed.

He blamed me. How could he not? I blamed myself.

"Look, when Colt gets worried, he gets in this zone. He locks down his feelings."

I swallowed. "I understand."

"I don't think you do. His father killed his mom."

"I know."

Kav looked surprised for a second. "Did you know he heard it all? He was hiding in a closet, and heard every shout and scream."

Oh, God.

"He blamed himself."

"He was a *child*."

"Doesn't matter to him. Then his sister's death just compounded it. He felt like he'd failed her."

"I've seen the way he drives himself to protect others. Especially Daisy."

Kav touched my hand, and I saw him frown. He could probably feel how cold my fingers were.

"I know he's afraid to lose the people he cares about," I said. "Like he did Chrissy."

Kav nodded, still frowning at me.

"He can't lose Daisy, Kavner."

"He won't. He has us, and we'll find her."

"He's lucky to have brothers like you." Someone to be there for him, no questions asked.

Kav tipped my chin up. "And he has you."

I looked at Colt's stiff back. He was leaning over the computer on the island. "I don't think he wants me right now. It's my fault Daisy is in danger."

"No, it's not." Kav's voice was sharp. "He's locked

down, Macy, it doesn't mean he doesn't care. He isn't used to having a woman, one he cares about. And it sure as hell doesn't mean he blames you. You aren't to blame for anything. Scott Warner did this. He's to blame."

I just stared at him.

"We found Warner's vehicle," Reath said.

"Got an address?" Colt barked. I saw him check his handgun and tuck it at his lower back.

"Yes," Reath replied.

"Let's go and get my daughter."

He strode to the stairs, and didn't look at me once.

My heart shriveled. Maybe my mom was right, after all. Maybe it was better to stay alone.

Kav rose. "We'll get Daisy back. It's going to be fine."

I managed a nod. "Yes. She'll be home. Safe."

All that mattered was that Daisy came home safely.

As the men all left, and I was standing there alone, an idea formed.

Maybe there was something I could do to bring Colt's daughter home.

37

COLT

Daisy was coming home. Whatever I had to do, I'd do it.

Reath hadn't let me drive. We were in one of his company SUVs, with Reath driving. Warner's vehicle had been spotted in Mid-City. The streets passed in a blur. Was Daisy scared? Hurting? My gut cramped. I couldn't fucking bear the thought.

I had to save her.

"Deep breath, Colt."

I glanced at Reath. "I'm fine."

"You're not fine," Dante said from the back seat.

"I just need to get her back."

"You've gone cold, I get that," Reath said.

"I'm fine. I'm just focused."

"You should've told Macy that," Kav muttered.

I frowned. Everything from the last thirty minutes was a blur. All I'd been focused on was getting Daisy's location. I had a vague memory of Macy's worried face.

"She's worried sick, and you treated her like she had an

infectious disease." Kav's voice sounded disapproving. "She thinks you blame her."

Everything inside me froze. "I don't blame her."

Kav cocked an eyebrow. "You should've told her that. She's blaming herself."

Fuck. I stared out the windshield. Kav was right. I knew how worried Macy would be about Daisy, and of course she'd blame herself.

I should have comforted her. Hell, I wasn't used to being part of a couple. I'd messed things up already.

"I'll tell her when we get back." I'd make it right, once my daughter was home safely.

"There." Reath pulled the SUV over. I saw the silver sedan parked on the street.

I was out before Reath turned off the engine. It only took two seconds to see the car was empty.

But I saw something on the seat.

An origami sunflower.

The one Macy had given to Daisy.

"He has her." I turned and looked down the street. But where the hell had he taken her?

Reath was on the phone, directing his team to search properties in the area.

I looked around, letting my instincts take over. I tried to mentally trace what Warner would've done when he'd gotten out of the truck.

"These are all family homes," I said. "Kids are at school, parents at work."

"Warner could hole up in one of them for a few hours," Beau said.

No. That didn't feel right. Warner thought he was smart, leading us on a chase. He felt superior.

"Reath, have your guys check for any cars reported stolen in the area over the last hour."

Reath's eyes widened minutely, and he nodded. "On it." He pressed the phone back to his ear. "Linc, I need you to check for—"

I looked around again. *I'm going to find you, Warner. Make you regret taking my girl and terrorizing my woman.*

My thoughts turned to Macy. When I got back, I'd make sure she knew exactly how I felt about her. So she never doubted it again.

"Okay. Blue Chevy Colorado. Got it."

I turned back to Reath.

My brother smiled briefly. "A blue Chevy truck was reported stolen thirty minutes ago. My guys are tracking it. It ran a red light about three blocks from here. Lincoln's doing a little less-than-legal hack into the car's GPS."

Energy filled me. *Gotcha, asshole.*

"Someone call Boone. He said he's happy to help out while he's in town." My mouth flattened. "Let's bring my daughter home, then I can get home to my woman."

"Your woman, huh?" Dante said.

"I'm not giving her up." My tone was as solid as granite. "She's mine."

Kav nodded. "Good. I didn't want to have to kick your ass if you messed it up."

"Let's save the ass-kicking for Warner," I said. "That bastard needs to learn a lesson."

Kav's smile held a deadly edge. "Yeah, don't mess with the Fury brothers."

38

MACY

As I slipped out of the warehouse, I scanned around. I didn't see any of Reath's security guards, but there was no one else around either.

Head down, I quickly marched toward the office, resolve filling me.

I was getting Daisy home safely. No matter what.

I turned the corner and half jogged to the office. I was out of breath as I unlocked the door and headed inside.

Colt. My mind kept going to him. I wondered if he was all right. He'd be so worried about Daisy.

My stomach lurched and I swallowed. He couldn't lose her.

I circled the desk and sat. Quickly, I opened my email and searched the trash folder. I saw the email from Scott and steeled myself. I made sure not to look at the gross pictures as I hit reply.

Tell me she's not hurt.

I hit send.

I pressed my palms to my eyes, all the emotions cutting through me like knives.

Ping.

My head jerked up. There was a reply.

She's fine.

I blew out a breath and typed.

Where are you? If I come to you, you have to let her go.

The reply was instantaneous.

I don't take orders from anyone.

God, he was a piece of work.

If I come, you let her go. A trade.

He waited a bit this time, every second making my nerves stretch tighter. A reply popped up.

Deal.

Okay. This was good. I could free Daisy and get her safe. My hands shook as I typed.

Where are you?

If you share where I am with the bounty hunter, the girl dies, Macy.

My hands shook even more.

Just me. Give me the address, Scott.

The address appeared and I tapped it into the map app on my phone. It wasn't far away. It looked like it was just a house. I quickly locked up the office and hurried back to the warehouse.

In the garage, my bike gleamed under the lights. I wheeled it out and pedaled off.

Get to Daisy. Get her free. That was all that mattered.

By the time I turned onto the street, my hands were hurting from gripping the handlebars so tightly.

Maybe my mom had been technically right about avoiding entanglements. It meant you avoided pain.

But it also meant you avoided the good stuff too. Happiness, joy, love.

I swallowed the lump in my throat. I loved Daisy. The little girl was sweet and caring, and she didn't deserve this.

And Colt... My heart thudded. He was grumpy and protective. He'd suffered, but he'd made a good life for himself, and he helped people.

I saw the house. There was a For Sale sign outside.

I parked my bike against the fence and pushed through the gate. The squeak as it opened grated along my nerves.

Daisy. The only thing I could focus on right now was Daisy.

As I neared the front door, it was wrenched open.

I stared at Scott. His scruff was way past needing a shave, and his mouth was a flat line. He looked like he hadn't been sleeping well.

"Get in here." He grabbed my arm, his fingers biting into my skin. I bit my lip.

He slammed the door closed behind me. The house was empty, with no furniture. He'd clearly broken in and had been hiding out here. It was probably why Colt and Reath hadn't been able to find him.

I didn't see Daisy. My pulse hammered. "Scott, where—?"

"Shut up." He swung me around and my shoulder hit the wall. Pain spiked across my upper back. "For once, you'll do as I say."

I lifted my chin. "Where is Daisy?"

"The brat is here." He hauled me through the room. "You shouldn't have left me, Macy. You should never run."

"I don't want to be with you, Scott." There was no longer any of the nice, easy-going man I'd met so many months ago. Maybe it had never been there. He'd certainly kept the controlling part of himself well hidden.

His gaze bored into mine, and he drew me up on my toes. "You're *mine*."

When Colt said those words, all I felt was a sense of rightness, a click as things fell into place. When Scott said it, it was like nails on a chalkboard. Wrong. So very wrong.

"I love you," he said. "You'll always be mine."

"I'm not yours, Scott. This isn't love. You need help. I don't love you, and I don't want to be with you."

"Be quiet!" he roared.

"Where's Daisy?" I raised my voice. "Daisy!"

I heard a muffled voice at the back of the house and yanked free of Scott.

"Daisy!"

When I entered the empty kitchen, I spotted Daisy huddled on the floor, her back to the cupboards. Relief shot through me. Her face was tear-stained, but she was otherwise unharmed.

"Daisy."

"Macy!"

I saw her face crumple. She launched herself at me and I caught her, hugging her hard.

"Where's Daddy?"

I swallowed. "Looking for you." Out of Scott's view, I handed her my cellphone. I lowered my voice. "I'm getting you out of here. When you're free, call him."

Her lips trembled. "What about you?"

My belly tied in knots. "Don't worry, sweetheart. I'll get out. I'll be right behind you. You just get to your dad."

She bit her bottom lip. "Macy—"

"Enough of the whispering," Scott barked.

I whirled to face him, pushing Daisy behind me.

"I've had enough of her." He pointed a finger at Daisy. "She bit me." He held up one hand.

I could see the nasty bite mark. *Good girl.* I squeezed her fingers. "You have me now. Let her go."

His gaze narrowed, a calculating gleam in them. "That asshole touched you. Kept you from me."

"I'm not a thing, Scott. I make my own decisions."

"You're *mine.* I want to make him pay for taking you." His gaze fell on Daisy.

Oh, no. Vicious protectiveness rushed through me. "Get ready to run," I murmured.

Daisy squeezed my fingers.

"This has to stop, Scott."

He laughed. "I'm in charge here. You will love me. We'll be together forever."

I wasn't letting him make me afraid anymore. I charged, and shoved him. He slammed into the wall.

"Run, Daisy!"

The little girl shot out of the room like a baby cheetah.

Scott bellowed, but I shoved him again. I wasn't letting him get her.

He pulled a fist back, then punched me in the stomach.

Oh, ow. That hurt. I doubled over, the air rushing out of me. It hurt to breathe.

"You never listen. You have to learn to listen, Macy." He clamped a hand around my throat. "You *will* love me."

Nothing mattered now. Daisy was free.

39

COLT

We found the Chevy truck abandoned in a side street. Boone had beaten us there and was standing beside it.

The tall man shook his head. "It's empty."

I kicked the front wheel and gritted my teeth.

"Easy." Beau gripped my shoulder.

"She's not here. My little girl is out there, somewhere, afraid."

"We are going to find her."

I managed a nod. My chest was so fucking tight. I saw Reath on his phone, frowning. I stiffened.

He finished the call and met my gaze.

"What?" I growled.

"Macy left the warehouse."

"Why?" Shit, I hadn't left any security for her.

"She stopped in at your office, sent some emails..." Reath's voice drifted off.

"Reath." I started to feel sick. "Tell me."

"Warner had sent her the same photos he'd left you on your vehicle."

"*Fuck.*"

"She deleted them. Protecting you, would be my guess."

I felt the pressure building behind my eyes. "And?"

"She used the email to contact Warner. Offered herself in trade for Daisy."

"Fucking hell." The ground moved under me. No. Warner was not sane when it came to Macy. "Where is she now?"

"He sent her an address. An empty house for sale on the edge of the Garden District."

Not far from here. I swiveled and headed for the SUV.

"I'll meet you there," Boone said.

Soon, although not soon enough for me, we were speeding toward the address. What the fuck had Macy been thinking?

She'd been thinking that I blamed her. Thinking that she could save Daisy.

I closed my eyes. If something happened to Macy, to either of them...

"Go faster, Reath."

My brother touched the console on the dash.

"Boss?" a deep voice said.

"Linc, need you to smooth the way for us."

"You got it."

Ahead, the traffic light turned green. The next one did the same. And the next one.

My cellphone rang and I saw Macy's name.

Thank fuck. My heart jumped. "Macy?"

"Daddy."

"Daisy, baby." My hand clenched on the phone. "Are you all right?"

"I got out." Her voice was shaky. "Daddy, Macy got me

out." A hiccupping sound. "He's got her. The bad man has Macy. She made me run."

Fuck. The plastic creaked in my grip. "Where are you?"

"I don't know. On a street."

"We're tracking the phone," Reath said. "She's near the address. Tell her to hide until she sees us."

"Daisy, find somewhere safe where the bad man can't see you. I'm coming."

"Okay. There's a fence." She paused. "Daddy, Macy—"

"I'm coming. I'm coming for you and Macy."

She let out a shuddering breath. "All right."

It was the longest drive of my life. I sucked in several deep breaths trying to stay calm.

Daisy was alone. And Warner had Macy.

I locked it down the best I could. My girls needed me.

Finally, Reath screeched to a halt. I leaped out of the SUV. Nearby, a black Ford Mustang pulled up and Boone climbed out.

"Daisy!"

My little girl flew out from behind a fence and sprinted toward me, her arms pumping.

I closed the distance and swept her into my arms.

Thank God.

"Daddy." She was crying. The tears rolling down her face killed me.

"You're safe now, short stuff. I've got you."

"I'm not afraid now." She pressed her small hands to my cheeks and stroked my beard. "I knew you'd come for me."

My heart swelled. "Always. We all will."

She shot me a tremulous smile and glanced at her uncles. Then her smile vanished. "You need to get Macy, Daddy."

"I know." I set her down. "Stay with Uncle Dante. I'm going to get Macy."

She nodded.

I kissed her cheek. "My brave girl." I handed her to Dante.

Over her head, my brother nodded. "Go get your woman. We'll be waiting for you."

I turned and eyed the house down the street.

"Plan?" Reath's face was set, focused.

"Reath, you, Kav, and Beau go around the back," I said. "Boone and I will go in the front."

Boone was former special forces. Exactly the man you wanted beside you in a fight. And I trusted my brothers to have my back and ensure Warner didn't get away.

My brothers nodded. No questions asked. Boone met my gaze and lifted his chin.

I'm coming, Macy.

40

MACY

My heart beat so loudly it was all I could hear.

"You're so stupid, Macy. You need to learn to listen." Scott's hands were still at my throat.

His fingers hurt where they dug into my skin, and my lungs burned.

But Daisy was free. Colt would find her. They'd be fine.

The two people I loved would be fine.

Oh, God. I loved Colton Fury. Every grumpy inch of him.

I looked into Scott's eyes. I wasn't sure what I'd once seen there. But as I stared at him, I vowed I wasn't going to die here, alone, in this vacant building.

I had a life to live, on my own terms. Not Scott's, not my mother's, mine.

I rammed my knee up between his legs. It was a decent hit, and Scott yelled, releasing me.

"You don't get to hurt me, asshole! Or dictate my life. I'm not stupid, and I don't need to learn anything. You do. You don't hit women. You don't kidnap little girls."

He made an ugly sound and charged me.

Oh, shit.

He hit me hard. We fell, both sprawled on the floor, and pain vibrated through me. I tried to turn, but he pinned me to the ground. A slap to the face stunned me. It hurt. Badly.

Dazed, I blinked up at him. He backhanded me again.

Then he caressed my cheek. "I do love you, Macy. You'll learn. I'll teach you."

I tasted blood in my mouth. "You have no idea what real love is."

He sneered. "You think you love that fucker you work for?"

"I do." I was afraid, but I let what I felt for Colt fill me.

And I hoped, despite everything, that he'd come for me.

I was tired of having no one.

Scott leaned down, his face an inch from mine, like he was going to kiss me. I turned my head to the side.

"I'll make you forget him." Then Scott's weight pushed off me.

Hope flared, and I tensed, ready to run.

But Scott sank a hand into my hair, and another twisted in my shirt.

"We're leaving. You'll forget this fucking city, and Fury."

He dragged me across the floor.

I kicked and struggled. I couldn't let him get me into a car. I knew if he got away with me, I'd never see Colt again.

I turned my head and sank my teeth into Scott's calf. He yelped and shook me.

"Do that again, and I'll kill you." His tone was like ice.

He was a monster.

Then he pulled a gun from the waistband of his pants, and my heart stopped.

41

COLT

Closing the distance to the house, I tried to find some control. A cool head.

But I couldn't.

Daisy was safe, but I knew Scott Warner would definitely hurt Macy.

I also knew my sunflower would fight him.

I stalked past the For Sale sign, and saw that the front door was ajar. Then from inside, I heard Macy cry out.

Boone grabbed my arm. "Steady. She needs you thinking, not getting yourself killed."

I nodded, and dragged in a deep breath, but I wasn't waiting any longer.

I moved silently up onto the porch. Boone was quiet behind me. He'd been trained. My brothers and I had learned to sneak around at a young age. Sometimes avoiding a beating had depended on it.

I peeked in the front window.

And my chest locked. Macy was on the floor, her mouth bleeding. I watched Warner draw a handgun.

"Gun." I spun and charged through the door.

In a smooth move, I pulled my own SIG, the metal cool in my hands. As a raced into the empty living area, I saw Macy launch herself at Warner. She tackled him around the knees.

The gun went off, the bullet hitting the ceiling. On the wood floor, Macy and Warner wrestled.

He still had the gun in his hand.

Fuck.

I aimed. "Put the gun down, Warner, or I will shoot you."

He didn't even react. Macy's head jerked up.

I saw that she was pissed, afraid, and running on adrenaline.

I wanted her safe, smiling, humming some godawful pop song.

Reath and Kavner burst in through the back door. Reath had his gun aimed, as well. Beau moved in behind them, blocking any escape through the back door.

"Put it down, Warner," I said again.

The man sat up, swiveling to aim at me.

I fired. He jerked, clamping a hand to his shoulder, his eyes wide. Then he turned the gun toward Macy.

I felt like the world slowed. As the barrel headed for Macy, my fucking heart stopped.

Boone came out of nowhere. He slammed a kick into Warner's arm, sending the gun flying. It crashed into the wall.

Macy scrambled backward.

"Kav," I barked.

"I've got her." My brother crouched beside Macy, pulling her into his arms.

I turned, my jaw tight, and closed the distance to Scott fucking Warner.

Boone had him pinned against the wall. His face was cool, set in a composed mask. I saw the soldier in him. I nodded and he stepped back.

Warner's gaze locked on me. "She's mine!"

"She was never yours." I gripped the front of his shirt. "First, she belongs to herself. And second, she's mine." I wound my fingers in the fabric, and saw fear break through Warner's eyes. "You took my daughter." I punched him in the face and he grunted. "You hurt my woman." I punched him again. "I won't let you hurt anyone else." I followed with a volley of brutal punches.

Warner cried out, blood pouring from his broken nose and split lip. I kept seeing the blood on Macy's mouth. I let my anger free, and I kept hitting him.

"That's enough, Colt." Reath appeared on my left. Beau appeared on my right.

"He's out cold," Beau said.

Warner became dead weight, his head lolling.

"I'd be doing everyone a favor if I kill him."

"And we'd have your back," Reath said. "But if you don't, he'll go away for a long time. Kidnapping. Stalking. Assault. Attempted murder." Reath lowered his voice. "And right now, your woman needs you. And your daughter's waiting to see that you're both okay."

Some of the raw fury leaked out of me. I glanced over at Macy. She sat in the circle of Kav's arms, watching me with wide eyes.

I stiffened. I expected to see fear or horror. I'd almost just beaten a man to death in front of her. She was trembling, but there was no fear.

When I turned toward her, she launched herself at me.

I caught her, sweeping her off her feet.

"Colt." As she buried herself against my chest, I breathed that berry scent deep.

"Fuck, Macy. I was so worried I'd be too late." That I'd fail her.

"I'm safe. I'm so sorry he took Daisy."

"That was *not* your fault." I cupped her cheeks, letting my gaze run over her poor, battered face. There was swelling, and bruises forming. "It's Warner's fault. I never blamed you, sunflower. I'm sorry you thought so."

Her lips trembled. She touched one of my hands. My knuckles were torn and bleeding. "We need to clean these up before Daisy sees the blood."

I nodded. I liked her looking out for me. "I was an asshole earlier, worried about Daisy, I locked everything in—"

"Because you always shoulder the blame that's not yours."

"Maybe." I gently kissed the unhurt side of her mouth. "Guess I've got a lot to learn about being in a relationship. Think you can help me with that?"

She gave me a small smile. "Maybe."

"You fucking turned my life upside down, Macy Underwood. From the first moment I hired you as my office assistant."

"Manager."

My lips quirked. "Manager. Now let's find Daisy, and get you both checked out."

42

MACY

As Dr. Hamilton finished probing my cheek, I tried not to wince.

But damn, it hurt.

"Sorry, young lady." The doctor stepped back. "Thankfully, there's nothing broken." There was sympathy in her brown eyes. "You'll need ice and some painkillers."

I nodded, and a second later Colt was there with an ice pack. He gently pressed it to my face. I had a few other aches and bruises, but I was alive. That was all that mattered.

Beside me on the couch, Daisy burrowed into my side. She hadn't left me since Colt had carried me out of that house.

I stroked her hair, knowing she needed the reassurance as much as I did.

And having her there, safe and warm, made me feel better.

Colt wrapped an arm around both of us. His brothers were sitting at the island, except for Reath, who was on the phone. The tall man, Boone, who looked like he should be in a Marvel movie was with them.

"Right." Dr. Hamilton closed her doctor's bag. "I'll send you boys my bill."

"You're on retainer," Reath said.

"Oh yes, that's right." The doctor winked at him. "Those of you with ladies, please keep them safe."

"We will," Dante said.

"And those of you without ladies need to find one."

"Well, I call dibs on you, Doc." Kav rose and offered the doctor his arm. "I'll walk you out."

"Gallant as always, Kavner Fury. And that charm doesn't fool me for a second." The doctor smiled. "One day, some woman is going to knock you off kilter."

Kav shook his head. "Hasn't happened yet."

"We'll see." The pair headed down the stairs.

Lola stepped forward. "I'm going to cook dinner. How about fajitas?"

"Lasagna," Daisy said.

The older woman smiled. "Lasagna it is."

"And garlic bread." Daisy lifted her head.

"Okay," Lola agreed.

"And homemade gelato."

I smiled. The kid was a Fury, through and through. Give them an inch, and they took a mile.

"Only if you help me make it," Lola said.

Daisy frowned and looked at me.

I tapped her nose. "Go on, gorgeous girl. I'll be right there. I'm not going anywhere."

She hesitated.

"I'll be with her," Colt told his daughter.

Daisy gripped my hand. "You saved me."

"Oh, Daisy." I cupped her cheeks. "I love you. I would do anything to keep you safe."

"I love you too, Macy." She hugged me hard, and I managed to hide my wince as she bumped some of my aching ribs.

I met Colt's gaze. There was so much warmth in it.

"Go." I tugged on Daisy's hair. "I want lasagna and gelato now, too."

Daisy hopped up and headed into the kitchen with Lola. His brothers and Boone were talking at the island.

"You love my daughter."

I looked at him. "She's easy to love. You're raising a good kid. And you're a hell of a dad."

"I didn't think I could do it. Single man, bounty hunter."

I took his hand and gave it a squeeze. But he wasn't done yet.

"And I'd fucked up with all the family I had."

"Hardly, Colt. Life isn't easy, and bad stuff happens. I might try to always look at the positive, but I know that things aren't always neat, simple, or pretty. You've suffered and survived a lot."

"Chrissy, my mom..."

"They made their choices. You did what you could. What happened to them was *not* your fault."

His lips twitched at the vehemence in my voice. "Okay, sunflower."

"I mean it, big guy. I'm not going to let you keep shouldering the blame."

He slid a hand into my hair. "Macy, I meant what I said. You've turned my life upside-down."

I smiled, ignoring the twinge in my swollen lip. "You haven't always been happy about that."

He made a sound. "I couldn't imagine it any other way now. Macy, I'm not letting you leave." He frowned. "I don't mean that the way Warner did."

A laugh escaped me. "I know."

"You want adventures, I'll give them to you."

Everything inside me warmed.

"You need pop music and flowers, I'll make it happen."

God, could you melt from happiness?

"Whatever you need, I'll get it for you."

"Colt, what happened to no complications and no strings?"

He hauled me onto his lap. "Fuck that. I want all your complications, all the strings. Tie those things around me and knot them as tight as you can."

I touched my hand to his jaw. "You're sure?"

"Yes. You make me happy, Macy. Even when I don't want to be."

My poor grump. "I'm gonna sing, dance, make you origami, put plants in your office, make you do paperwork."

"I want all of that." A faint scowl appeared. "Except for the paperwork."

"Tough, you're getting it. And my care, and my love."

He sucked in a breath.

"Scary, huh?" I whispered.

"No." He shook his head. "I want your love, because I love you too, Macy."

He said the words fast.

Oh. Tears welled in my eyes. Colton Fury loved me. I could barely breathe.

"I want to love you, take care of you, give you everything you need. Forever. Until we're both old and gray. Until I turn to dust."

I smiled. "I just need you. And Daisy."

He kissed me. He was careful not to bump where I was sore.

My grumpy bounty hunter could be gentle.

Yes, my mom had been wrong.

Sometimes things were forever.

43

COLT

Having Macy on my lap, clinging to me as I kissed her, eased the last of my ragged nerves.

She and Daisy were safe.

Macy loved me.

"Stay. With me." I murmured the words against her lips.

"I will."

"Make a home with us."

"It already feels like home," she murmured back.

I wrenched my lips free, my hands clamped on her thighs. I raised my voice. "Lola, you and Daisy won't have dinner ready for a while, right?"

"About an hour," Lola answered.

"Good." I rose with Macy in my arms.

She squeaked, and ran her arm along my shoulders.

"I need to check Macy's wounds and...put more ice on them."

I heard my brothers all snort as I strode out.

"He keeps ice in his bedroom?" Boone asked, as the others chuckled.

I strode to the entrance to my place. It only took me a minute to close the distance to my bedroom.

I sat on the bed, and set Macy on her feet in front of me.

My heart was thumping. Shadows and light danced over her.

"I need you." It was something I'd never, ever said to a woman in my life. "I need to be inside you."

Her lips curved as I unbuttoned her shirt. She pushed it off and together we unfastened her pants. She quickly ditched her bra and panties.

God, she was so beautiful.

She gripped my Henley, and we pulled it over my head. Then I opened my jeans. My cock was already hard and throbbing.

Macy took several fast breaths. "I need you, Colt."

I'd never, ever get tired of hearing that. "You want my cock, sunflower? Deep inside you?"

"Yes."

I pulled her to me, and she straddled me. Gritting my teeth, I stroked between her legs, checking that she was ready. She was already slick.

"Shit, Macy."

She rubbed against my hand. "Hurry."

Her hands curved over my shoulders. I reached for my cock, guiding it right where we both wanted it.

Then Macy sank down, taking all of my hard cock in one powerful move. She cried out, and I gave a strangled groan.

So fucking good. Like sliding home.

"It's never enough," I growled, filling my palms with her ass. "I'll never get enough of you."

She started to ride me. I pumped my hips up, meeting her drives.

I wrapped my arms around her, pulling her mouth to mine. I wanted to be closer, as close as I could.

As I thrust my cock inside her, she pulled her mouth free and chanted my name. Our flesh slapped together as she moved faster.

"Oh, God. Colt... It's... I'm coming."

"Good. I want you to come for me."

"Together."

"Yes, let me feel it."

I felt her inner muscles tighten, then she was coming. She cried out, and my fingers dug into the flesh of her ass.

"*Christ.*" I thrust up, my own climax ripped out of me. I shoved her down on my lap, filling her.

Waves of pleasure shook my bones, and she leaned down, sinking her teeth into my shoulder.

Spent, I fell back on the bed, taking her with me.

"That was..." Her breath puffed against my chest.

"I know." I felt wrung dry. "All I can think of is fuck. Just fuck."

She giggled and kissed my pec. "Very profound, Colt."

"I'm a bounty hunter. Profound is not in my vocabulary." I tipped her face up. Just looking at her made me feel so much. "You're getting rid of your house."

"Am I?"

"Yes. You're moving in here. For good."

"I'm not sure I can live with my boss. It's inappropriate." Her voice held a teasing tone.

"Fuck inappropriate. You'll also be fucking your boss on your lunch breaks."

She burst out laughing. "You're still not getting out of the paperwork, though."

I groaned. "Fine, sex with my beautiful office assistant... I mean, office manager, will help me cope."

Playfully, she slapped me.

I cupped her swollen cheek.

"I'm okay," she said. "I'm so far past okay it's not funny. I love you, Colt. I love you like this, relaxed and naked. Intense and grumpy. And sweet and loving."

I frowned. "I'm not sweet."

"Sometimes."

"No, I'm not."

She smacked a kiss to my lips and sat up. "Come on, big guy. We have lasagna to eat."

44

COLT

A few weeks later

"I can't believe we're having a picnic," Beau rumbled.

I bit into a sandwich. "It was Macy's idea, and Daisy was one hundred percent behind it."

"And whatever Macy and Daisy want, you give it to them."

"Yep." I glanced over to where my girls were running across the grass with a kite. They hadn't managed to get it in the air yet, but they were still having fun. We were at Audubon Park in Uptown. Macy had wanted to have a "goodbye to summer" picnic.

My gaze snagged on her legs. She was wearing tiny shorts that had me imagining sliding them off her later. We were officially living together. We'd moved all her stuff in. She'd already added throw cushions to the couch, more furniture, vases filled with flowers, and other stuff. She was making it a home.

Ours.

I nudged the picnic basket closer to Beau. He was lounging on the picnic blanket beside me. "There's some of Lola's fried chicken in there. Enjoy some food and quit bitching."

Beau loved Lola's fried chicken. Without a word, he dug in.

I spotted Mila and Dante walking under some oak trees nearby, holding hands. I couldn't remember ever seeing my brother so happy. I got it now.

My gaze went back to Macy and Daisy. Kav was with them, trying to get the kite in the air. So far they'd spent more time running around. He was wearing khaki shorts and a loose, white linen shirt. Even when he was dressed in casual gear, he still looked rich. I made a mental note to give him hell about it later.

"Happy?"

Reath appeared from nowhere beside me. "Yeah. I am."

"So being in a relationship is worth the risk."

"It is. It's not always easy." When Macy noticed me looking at her, she smiled. Every time I saw her smile, it lit things up inside me. I was whipped and I didn't care one bit. "She fucking holds my heart in her hands. It's as scary as hell."

"She looks sweet," Reath said, "but she'll protect it fiercely."

"I know." And it was my job to keep her happy. And safe.

I'd do whatever I had to do to keep both my girls smiling, singing, and giggling.

I saw Macy reach out and ruffle Daisy's hair. She loved my little girl. And I loved that Daisy had someone else in her life who would be there for her. Always.

"You and Macy going to give Daisy a little brother or sister?" Beau asked.

"What?" I felt like I'd been hit with an electric shock.

Beau grinned over some chicken. "Don't tell me you hadn't thought about it?"

I hadn't. I'd just been so wrapped up in Macy that I hadn't thought past having her in my place, in my bed. I felt a bit lightheaded as I watched her. Instantly, I could picture her round with a baby. My baby.

Shit. Fuck.

"He looks like you punched him with your famous Beauden Fury combo." Reath sounded amused.

"We have time." But yeah, I wanted a baby. One we'd make together. Daisy would love it, and be a brilliant big sister.

Leaving my brothers, I headed across the grass. Kav was untangling the kite string from around Daisy's legs. My daughter was giggling. I slipped an arm around Macy and kissed her.

"I told you a picnic was an excellent idea," she said.

"My brothers weren't convinced at first. I think Lola's fried chicken won them over."

"And you?" She pressed her hands to my chest.

"As long as I'm with you, I don't care where we are."

She smiled. "You say the sweetest things."

I saw Kav straighten. He was glancing down one of the paths, frowning. I followed his gaze, and spotted a tall woman striding down the path. She wore fitted black pants and a sleeveless white shirt. She walked with purpose. A woman on a mission.

Her gaze was locked on Kavner.

Kav stared back.

I frowned. "Dai, go get some fried chicken before Uncle Beau eats it all."

"Yum." She ran off, dragging the kite behind her.

"Friend of yours?" I asked my brother.

"Not really."

The woman got closer, and I raised a brow. She had smooth brown skin, and striking features. Her long, black hair was in a ponytail.

"Mr. Fury."

"Treasury Agent Coleman. Fancy meeting you here." Kav smiled. "Are you here for a picnic?"

Treasury agent? I watched the woman carefully. I pegged her as smart, driven, and with a hard on for Kav.

And not in the usual way women wanted my brother.

"Don't tell me you're working on a Sunday," Kav continued.

"I was just in the neighborhood," Agent Coleman said. "And I'm always working."

"It's not good for your stress levels. You have to learn to live a little."

The agent stepped closer. "You know I'm here to uncover money laundering, Fury. And I know you're tied up in it. I *will* find the evidence I need."

Kav sighed. "I'm a legitimate businessman, London. Everything I own is above board."

"That's Treasury Agent Coleman to you, Mr. Fury."

My gaze narrowed. Kav's businesses were legal now, although they'd had a few...gray areas when he'd first started out.

"Hi, I'm Macy." My woman stepped forward, grinning.

The agent blinked. "Hello."

"Would you like to join us for a picnic?"

Kav's brows went up. I scowled at Macy. What was she up to?

"I promise you that Kavner is a good man," Macy said. "You just need to get to know him."

Agent Coleman straightened. "Sorry, I have to go." She shot a glare at Kav.

My brother smiled at her.

Then the agent stalked off on her long legs.

"What did you do to piss her off?" I asked.

"Nothing." Kav was still watching her walk away. "Yet."

"But you've met before."

Kav's lips curled. "Oh, yes. The lovely agent and I have crossed paths." Then he turned. "I need some fried chicken, and a glass of that Chardonnay I brought."

I watched him cast one last glance at the agent before he headed toward the picnic blanket.

Macy stood there grinning at Kav's back.

"What's going on in that head of yours, sunflower." I squeezed the back of her neck.

"Did you see the way Kav watched her? And the way she stood up to him? She didn't fawn or simper all over him like most women do."

My eyebrows went up. "You think my brother likes the treasury agent who's clearly out to get him?"

"Yep."

That was my Macy, always looking for the good in things.

She snuggled in against my side. "Now, how about a quick walk around the fountain—" she lowered her voice "—so I can kiss you out of view of everybody?"

I smiled. "Sounds good to me."

She could ask me anything, and I'd give it to her.

45

MACY

Carrying my cute little watering can, I watered the plants around the office.

Life was...amazing. I poured some water on my favorite orchid. Being with Colt was not all unicorns and rainbows. He was still my grump, and we were learning to live together—two people used to doing things our own way.

I smiled and set the can down on my desk. Colt was learning to compromise, and I loved coaxing smiles out of my grumpy bounty hunter. It was Daisy I'd been worried about, but needlessly, as it turned out. The little girl had accepted my presence in their home with a beaming smile.

The only downside to my amazing life this week was that Colt was away. He'd been called up for a job in Texas.

But I knew he'd come home to us when he was done. While he was away, Lola, Colt's brothers, and Mila made sure we were never alone.

It felt nice to have a home filled with laughter, people, and warmth.

And love.

"Mom, I found the best adventure of all." I smiled. I

knew she'd be happy for me. "He's perfect for me. We balance each other out."

The office door opened, and I whirled.

Colt filled the doorway—as hot as always in well-worn jeans and a black Henley.

"You're home!" I ran and leaped.

He caught me, smiling down at me.

Then he kissed me.

Mmm. I threw my arms around his neck and kissed him back.

When I finally pulled back, I was out of breath. I nibbled his ear. "I thought you'd be gone longer. You've only been gone three days. I mean, I'm glad you're home. I missed you."

His big hands cupped my ass. "I missed you too. I had motivation to catch the bad guy fast and get home to my girls."

Warmth bloomed inside me. My sweet grump.

He bit my bottom lip and made me shiver. "And now, my sexy little assistant is going to welcome the boss back. Enthusiastically. On his desk."

"Really?" I batted my eyelashes. "I'm not sure that's appropriate."

"Oh, it's going to be very inappropriate." He flipped the lock on the front door, and carried me into his office.

I pressed my mouth to his neck, scraping my teeth over his skin. Desire coiled inside me. I felt so very blessed. I had this amazing hot guy who wanted me. An amazing man I loved, and who loved me back.

I didn't need to travel, or experience new things and places. This right here, Colt, was all I needed.

He paused at his desk and raised a brow.

I grinned. "I got you a gift." A new cactus rested in a

bright pot covered in sequins and glitter. "Daisy decorated the pot for you."

"But I can see your influence."

My grin widened. There was a grumpy origami bear scaling the cactus. "How could you tell?"

"Naughty girls get punished, sunflower." He set me on the desk.

"Oh, I hope so."

He sat in his chair in front of me, then cupped my face. The look in his eyes made me melt.

"I love you so fucking much."

Oh. I melted a little more. "I love you too, big guy. More than I ever thought possible."

He reached into his pocket and held out some red paper.

"Colt." My heart squeezed. It was a red origami heart. Terribly made.

"You already have my heart, Macy. I know it was a little battered—"

"It's perfect, and so's this one." I took the paper heart, then placed my palm over the one in his chest. It beat steadily under my fingers. "And I'll take care of this. I promise." I reached up and toyed with the tie on my halter top. "Now, you mentioned being inappropriate, Mr. Fury?"

He smiled. "So I did." With one tug, he untied my top and pushed it down. I was wearing the pink lace bra that I knew he loved.

He growled.

"I love that sound."

"I love your breasts." He cupped them. "And your legs, and your toes, your ears, and your neck. Pretty much all of you."

"Since you're a man of action, I think you'd better show me just how much you love me."

His lips quirked, and as always, I loved that smile.

"My pleasure, sunflower. My pleasure."

But as he pushed me back on his desk, his mouth on mine, I knew the pleasure would belong to both of us.

I hope you enjoyed Colt and Macy's story!

The Fury Brothers continues with *Burn*, starring billionaire Kavner Fury and the Treasury Agent who's out to get him. Coming 2024.

If you'd like to know more about **Boone Hendrix**, he's made cameos in both the Billionaire Series and Sentinel Security series. His story, *The Hero She Needs*, is coming in December 2023, the first book in my new series, **Unbroken Heroes**.

For more action-packed romance, check out the first book in the **Billionaire Heists**, *Stealing from Mr. Rich* (Monroe and Zane's story). **Read on for a preview of the first chapter.**

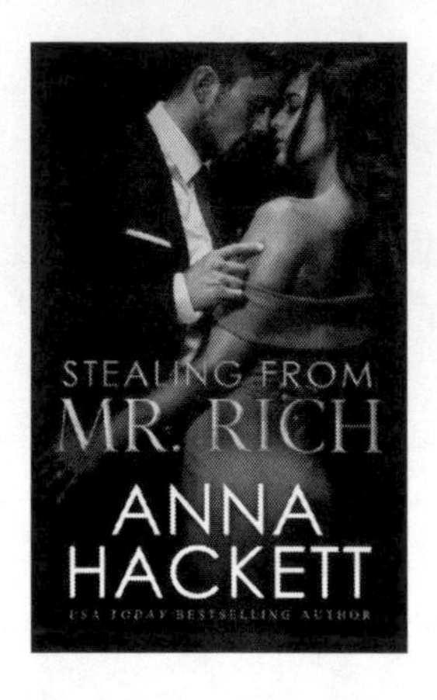

Don't miss out! For updates about new releases, free books, and other fun stuff, sign up for my VIP mailing list and get your *free box set* containing three action-packed romances.

Visit here to get started: www.annahackett.com

Would you like a FREE BOX SET of my books?

PREVIEW: STEALING FROM MR. RICH

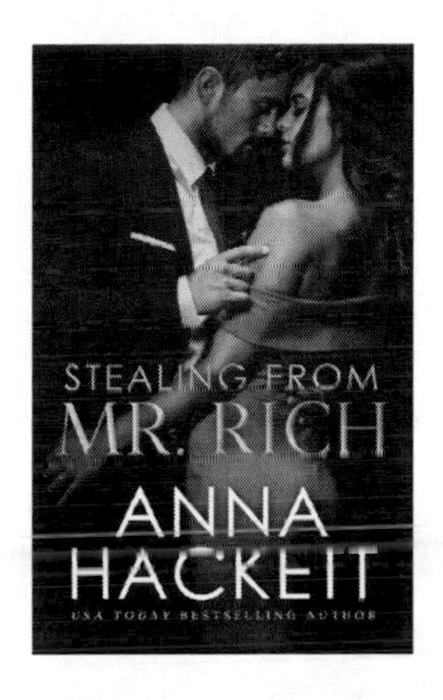

Brother in Trouble

Monroe

The old-fashioned Rosengrens safe was a beauty.

I carefully turned the combination dial, then pressed closer to the safe. The metal was cool under my fingertips. The safe wasn't pretty, but stout and secure. There was something to be said for solid security.

Rosengrens had started making safes in Sweden over a hundred years ago. They were good at it. I listened to the pins, waiting for contact. Newer safes had internals made from lightweight materials to reduce sensory feedback, so I didn't get to use these skills very often.

Some people could play the piano, I could play a safe. The tiny vibration I was waiting for reached my fingertips, followed by the faintest click.

"I've gotcha, old girl." The Rosengrens had quite a few quirks, but my blood sang as I moved the dial again.

I heard a louder click and spun the handle.

The safe door swung open. Inside, I saw stacks of jewelry cases and wads of hundred-dollar bills. *Nice.*

Standing, I dusted my hands off on my jeans. "There you go, Mr. Goldstein."

"You are a doll, Monroe O'Connor. Thank you."

The older man, dressed neatly in pressed chinos and a blue shirt, grinned at me. He had coke-bottle glasses, wispy, white hair, and a wrinkled face.

I smiled at him. Mr. Goldstein was one of my favorite people. "I'll send you my bill."

His grin widened. "I don't know what I'd do without you."

I raised a brow. "You could stop forgetting your safe combination."

The wealthy old man called me every month or so to open his safe. Right now, we were standing in the home office of his expensive Park Avenue penthouse.

It was decorated in what I thought of as "rich, old man." There were heavy drapes, gold-framed artwork, lots of dark wood—including the built-in shelves around the safe—and a huge desk.

"Then I wouldn't get to see your pretty face," he said.

I smiled and patted his shoulder. "I'll see you next month, Mr. Goldstein." The poor man was lonely. His wife had died the year before, and his only son lived in Europe.

"Sure thing, Monroe. I'll have some of those donuts you like."

We headed for the front door and my chest tightened. I understood feeling lonely. "You could do with some new locks on your door. I mean, your building has top-notch security, but you can never be too careful. Pop by the shop if you want to talk locks."

He beamed at me and held the door open. "I might do that."

"Bye, Mr. Goldstein."

I headed down the plush hall to the elevator. Everything in the building screamed old money. I felt like an imposter just being in the building. Like I had "daughter of a criminal" stamped on my head.

Pulling out my cell phone, I pulled up my accounting app and entered Mr. Goldstein's callout. Next, I checked my messages.

Still nothing from Maguire.

Frowning, I bit my lip. That made it three days since I'd heard from my little brother. I shot him off a quick text.

"Text me back, Mag," I muttered.

The elevator opened and I stepped in, trying not to worry about Maguire. He was an adult, but I'd practically raised him. Most days it felt like I had a twenty-four-year-old kid.

The elevator slowed and stopped at another floor. An older, well-dressed couple entered. They eyed me and my well-worn jeans like I'd crawled out from under a rock.

I smiled. "Good morning."

Yeah, yeah, I'm not wearing designer duds, and my bank

account doesn't have a gazillion zeros. You're so much better than me.

Ignoring them, I scrolled through Instagram. When we finally reached the lobby, the couple shot me another dubious look before they left. I strode out across the marble-lined space and rolled my eyes.

During my teens, I'd cared about what people thought. Everyone had known that my father was Terry O'Connor—expert thief, safecracker, and con man. I'd felt every repulsed look and sly smirk at high school.

Then I'd grown up, cultivated some thicker skin, and learned not to care. *Fuck 'em.* People who looked down on others for things outside their control were assholes.

I wrinkled my nose. Okay, it was easier said than done.

When I walked outside, the street was busy. I smiled, breathing in the scent of New York—car exhaust, burnt meat, and rotting trash. Besides, most people cared more about themselves. They judged you, left you bleeding, then forgot you in the blink of an eye.

I unlocked my bicycle, and pulled on my helmet, then set off down the street. I needed to get to the store. The ride wasn't long, but I spent every second worrying about Mag.

My brother had a knack for finding trouble. I sighed. After a childhood, where both our mothers had taken off, and Da was in and out of jail, Mag was entitled to being a bit messed up. The O'Connors were a long way from the Brady Bunch.

I pulled up in front of my shop in Hell's Kitchen and stopped for a second.

I grinned. *All mine.*

Okay, I didn't own the building, but I owned the store. The sign above the shop said *Lady Locksmith.* The logo was lipstick red—a woman's hand with gorgeous red nails, holding a set of keys.

After I locked up my bike, I strode inside. A chime sounded.

God, I loved the place. It was filled with glossy, warm-wood shelves lined with displays of state-of-the-art locks and safes. A key-cutting machine sat at the back.

A blonde head popped up from behind a long, shiny counter.

"You're back," Sabrina said.

My best friend looked like a doll—small, petite, with a head of golden curls.

We'd met doing our business degrees at college, and had become fast friends. Sabrina had always wanted to be tall and sexy, but had to settle for small and cute. She was my manager, and was getting married in a month.

"Yeah, Mr. Goldstein forgot his safe code again," I said.

Sabrina snorted. "That old coot doesn't forget, he just likes looking at your ass."

"He's harmless. He's nice, and lonely. How's the team doing?"

Sabrina leaned forward, pulling out her tablet. I often wondered if she slept with it. "Liz is out back unpacking stock." Sabrina's nose wrinkled. "McRoberts overcharged us on the Schlage locks again."

"That prick." He was always trying to screw me over. "I'll call him."

"Paola, Kat, and Isabella are all out on jobs."

Excellent. Business was doing well. Lady Locksmith specialized in providing female locksmiths to all the single ladies of New York. They also advised on how to keep them safe—securing locks, doors, and windows.

I had a dream of one day seeing multiple Lady Locksmiths around the city. Hell, around every city. A girl could dream. Growing up, once I understood the damage my father did to other people, all I'd wanted was to be respectable. To earn my own way and add to the world, not take from it.

"Did you get that new article I sent you to post on the blog?" I asked.

Sabrina nodded. "It'll go live shortly, and then I'll post on Insta, as well."

When I had the time, I wrote articles on how women—single *and* married—should secure their homes. My latest was aimed at domestic-violence survivors, and helping them feel safe. I donated my time to Nightingale House, a local shelter that helped women leaving DV situations, and I installed locks for them, free of charge.

"We should start a podcast," Sabrina said.

I wrinkled my nose. "I don't have time to sit around recording stuff." I did my fair share of callouts for jobs, plus at night I had to stay on top of the business-side of the store.

"Fine, fine." Sabrina leaned against the counter and eyed my jeans. "Damn, I hate you for being tall, long, and gorgeous. You're going to look *way* too beautiful as my maid of honor." She waved a hand between us. "You're all tall, sleek, and dark-haired, and I'm...the opposite."

I had some distant Black Irish ancestor to thank for my pale skin and ink-black hair. Growing up, I wanted to be short, blonde, and tanned. I snorted. "Beauty comes in all different forms, Sabrina." I gripped her shoulders. "You are so damn pretty, and your fiancé happens to think you are the most beautiful woman in the world. Andrew is gaga over you."

Sabrina sighed happily. "He does and he is." A pause.

"So, do you have a date for my wedding yet?" My bestie's voice turned breezy and casual.

Uh-oh. I froze. All the wedding prep had sent my normally easygoing best friend a bit crazy. And I knew very well not to trust that tone.

I edged toward my office. "Not yet."

Sabrina's blue eyes sparked. "It's only *four* weeks away, Monroe. The maid of honor can't come alone."

"I'll be busy helping you out—"

"Find a date, Monroe."

"I don't want to just pick anyone for your wedding—"

Sabrina stomped her foot. "Find someone, or I'll find someone for you."

I held up my hands. "Okay, okay." I headed for my office. "I'll—" My cell phone rang. *Yes.* "I've got a call. Got to go." I dove through the office door.

"I won't forget," Sabrina yelled. "I'll revoke your best-friend status, if I have to."

I closed the door on my bridezilla bestie and looked at the phone.

Maguire. Finally.

I stabbed the call button. "Where have you been?"

"We have your brother," a robotic voice said.

My blood ran cold. My chest felt like it had filled with concrete.

"If you want to keep him alive, you'll do exactly as I say."

Zane

God, this party was boring.

Zane Roth sipped his wine and glanced around the ballroom at the Mandarin Oriental. The party held the Who's Who of New York society, all dressed up in their glittering best. The ceiling shimmered with a sea of crystal lights, tall flower arrangements dominated the tables, and the wall of windows had a great view of the Manhattan skyline.

Everything was picture perfect...and boring.

If it wasn't for the charity auction, he wouldn't be dressed in his tuxedo and dodging annoying people.

"I'm so sick of these parties," he muttered.

A snort came from beside him.

One of his best friends, Maverick Rivera, sipped his wine. "You were voted New York's sexiest billionaire bachelor. You should be loving this shindig."

Mav had been one of his best friends since college. Like Zane, Maverick hadn't come from wealth. They'd both earned it the old-fashioned way. Zane loved numbers and money, and had made Wall Street his hunting ground. Mav was a geek, despite not looking like a stereotypical one. He'd grown up in a strong, Mexican-American family, and with his brown skin, broad shoulders, and the fact that he worked out a lot, no one would pick him for a tech billionaire.

But under the big body, the man was a computer geek to the bone.

"All the society mamas are giving you lots of speculative looks." Mav gave him a small grin.

"Shut it, Rivera."

"They're all dreaming of marrying their daughters off to billionaire Zane Roth, the finance King of Wall Street."

Zane glared. "You done?"

"Oh, I could go on."

"I seem to recall another article about the billionaire bachelors. All three of us." Zane tipped his glass at his friend. "They'll be coming for you, next."

Mav's smile dissolved, and he shrugged a broad shoulder. "I'll toss Kensington at them. He's pretty."

Liam Kensington was the third member of their trio. Unlike Zane and Mav, Liam had come from money, although he worked hard to avoid his bloodsucking family.

Zane saw a woman in a slinky, blue dress shoot him a welcoming smile.

He looked away.

When he'd made his first billion, he'd welcomed the attention. Especially the female attention. He'd bedded more than his fair share of gorgeous women.

Of late, nothing and no one caught his interest. Women all left him feeling numb.

Work. He thrived on that.

A part of him figured he'd never find a woman who made him feel the same way as his work.

"Speak of the devil," Mav said.

Zane looked up to see Liam Kensington striding toward them. With the lean body of a swimmer, clad in a perfectly tailored tuxedo, he looked every inch the billionaire. His gold hair complemented a face the ladies oohed over.

People tried to get his attention, but the real estate mogul ignored everyone.

He reached Zane and Mav, grabbed Zane's wine, and emptied it in two gulps.

"I hate this party. When can we leave?" Having spent his formative years in London, he had a posh British accent. Another thing the ladies loved. "I have a contract to work on, my fundraiser ball to plan, and things to catch up on after our trip to San Francisco."

The three of them had just returned from a business trip to the West Coast.

"Can't leave until the auction's done," Zane said.

Liam sighed. His handsome face often had him voted the best-looking billionaire bachelor.

"Buy up big," Zane said. "Proceeds go to the Boys and Girls Clubs."

"One of your pet charities," Liam said.

"Yeah." Zane's father had left when he was seven. His mom had worked hard to support them. She was his hero. He liked to give back to charities that supported kids growing up in tough circumstances.

He'd set his mom up in a gorgeous house Upstate that she loved. And he was here for her tonight.

"Don't bid on the Phillips-Morley necklace, though," he added. "It's mine."

The necklace had a huge, rectangular sapphire pendant surrounded by diamonds. It was the real-life necklace said to have inspired the necklace in the movie, *Titanic*. It had been given to a young woman, Kate Florence Phillips, by her lover, Henry Samuel Morley. The two had run away together and booked passage on the Titanic.

Unfortunately for poor Kate, Henry had drowned when the ship had sunk. She'd returned to England with the necklace and a baby in her belly.

Zane's mother had always loved the story and pored over pictures of the necklace. She'd told him the story of the lovers, over and over.

"It was a gift from a man to a woman he loved. She was a shop girl, and he owned the store, but they fell in love, even though society frowned on their love." She sighed.

"That's true love, Zane. Devotion, loyalty, through the good times and the bad."

Everything Carol Roth had never known.

Of course, it turned out old Henry was much older than his lover, and already married. But Zane didn't want to ruin the fairy tale for his mom.

Now, the Phillips-Morley necklace had turned up, and was being offered at auction. And Zane was going to get it for his mom. It was her birthday in a few months.

"Hey, is your fancy, new safe ready yet?" Zane asked Mav.

His friend nodded. "You're getting one of the first ones. I can have my team install it this week."

"Perfect." Mav's new Riv3000 was the latest in high-tech safes and said to be unbreakable. "I'll keep the necklace in it until my mom's birthday."

Someone called out Liam's name. With a sigh, their friend forced a smile. "Can't dodge this one. Simpson's an investor in my Brooklyn project. I'll be back."

"Need a refill?" Zane asked Mav.

"Sure."

Zane headed for the bar. He'd almost reached it when a manicured hand snagged his arm.

"Zane."

He looked down at the woman and barely swallowed his groan. "Allegra. You look lovely this evening."

She did. Allegra Montgomery's shimmery, silver dress hugged her slender figure, and her cloud of mahogany brown hair accented her beautiful face. As the only daughter of a wealthy New York family—her father was from *the* Montgomery family and her mother was a former Miss America—Allegra was well-bred and well-educated but also, as he'd discovered, spoiled and liked getting her way.

Her dark eyes bored into him. "I'm sorry things ended badly for us the other month. I was..." Her voice lowered, and she stroked his forearm. "I miss you. I was hoping we could catch up again."

Zane arched a brow. They'd dated for a few weeks, shared a few dinners, and some decent sex. But Allegra liked being the center of attention, complained that he worked too much, and had constantly hounded him to take her on vacation. Preferably on a private jet to Tahiti or the Maldives.

When she'd asked him if it would be too much for him to give her a credit card of her own, for monthly expenses, Zane had exited stage left.

"I don't think so, Allegra. We aren't...compatible."

Her full lips turned into a pout. "I thought we were *very* compatible."

He cleared his throat. "I heard you moved on. With Chip Huffington."

Allegra waved a hand. "Oh, that's nothing serious."

And Chip was only a millionaire. Allegra would see that as a step down. In fact, Zane felt like every time she looked at him, he could almost see little dollar signs in her eyes.

He dredged up a smile. "I wish you all the best, Allegra. Good evening." He sidestepped her and made a beeline for the bar.

"What can I get you?" the bartender asked.

Wine wasn't going to cut it. It would probably be frowned on to ask for an entire bottle of Scotch. "Two glasses of Scotch, please. On the rocks. Do you have Macallan?"

"No, sorry, sir. Will Glenfiddich do?"

"Sure."

"Ladies and gentlemen," a voice said over the loudspeaker. The lights lowered. "I hope you're ready to spend big for a wonderful cause."

Carrying the drinks, Zane hurried back to Mav and Liam. He handed Mav a glass.

"Let's do this," Mav grumbled. "And next time, I'll make a generous online donation so I don't have to come to the party."

"Drinks at my place after I get the necklace," Zane said. "I have a very good bottle of Macallan."

Mav stilled. "How good?"

"Macallan 25. Single malt."

"I'm there," Liam said.

Mav lifted his chin.

Ahead, Zane watched the evening's host lift a black cloth off a pedestal. He stared at the necklace, the sapphire glittering under the lights.

There it was.

The sapphire was a deep, rich blue. Just like all the photos his mother had shown him.

"Get that damn necklace, Roth, and let's get out of here," Mav said.

Zane nodded. He'd get the necklace for the one woman in his life who rarely asked for anything, then escape the rest of the bloodsuckers and hang with his friends.

Billionaire Heists

Stealing from Mr. Rich

Blackmailing Mr. Bossman

Hacking Mr. CEO

PREVIEW: NORCROSS SECURITY

Want more action-packed romance? Then check out the men of **Norcross Security**.

The only man who can keep her safe is her boss' gorgeous brother.

Museum curator Haven McKinney has sworn off men. All of them. Totally. She's recently escaped a bad ex and started a new life for herself in San Francisco. She *loves* her job at the Hutton Museum, likes her new boss, and has made best friends with his feisty sister. Haven's also desperately trying *not* to notice their brother: hotshot investigator Rhys Norcross. And she's *really* trying not to notice his muscular body, sexy tattoos, and charming smile.

Nope, Rhys is off limits. But then Haven finds herself in the middle of a deadly situation...

Investigator Rhys Norcross is good at finding his targets. After leaving an elite Ghost Ops military team, the former Delta Force soldier thrives on his job at his brother's security firm, Norcross Security. He's had his eye on smart, sexy Haven for a while, but the pretty curator with her eyes full of secrets is proving far harder to chase down than he anticipated.

Luckily, Rhys never, ever gives up.

When thieves target the museum and steal a multimillion-dollar painting in a daring theft, Haven finds herself in trouble, and dangers from her past rising. Rhys vows to do whatever it takes to keep her safe, and Haven finds herself risking the one thing she was trying so hard to protect—her heart.

Norcross Security

The Investigator
The Troubleshooter
The Specialist
The Bodyguard
The Hacker
The Powerbroker
The Detective
The Medic
The Protector
Also Available as Audiobooks!

ALSO BY ANNA HACKETT

Fury Brothers

Fury

Sentinel Security

Wolf

Hades

Striker

Steel

Excalibur

Hex

Also Available as Audiobooks!

Norcross Security

The Investigator

The Troubleshooter

The Specialist

The Bodyguard

The Hacker

The Powerbroker

The Detective

The Medic

The Protector

Also Available as Audiobooks!

Billionaire Heists

Stealing from Mr. Rich

Blackmailing Mr. Bossman

Hacking Mr. CEO

Also Available as Audiobooks!

Team 52

Mission: Her Protection

Mission: Her Rescue

Mission: Her Security

Mission: Her Defense

Mission: Her Safety

Mission: Her Freedom

Mission: Her Shield

Mission: Her Justice

Also Available as Audiobooks!

Treasure Hunter Security

Undiscovered

Uncharted

Unexplored

Unfathomed

Untraveled

Unmapped

Unidentified

Undetected

Also Available as Audiobooks!

Oronis Knights

Knightmaster

Knighthunter

Galactic Kings

Overlord

Emperor

Captain of the Guard

Conqueror

Also Available as Audiobooks!

Eon Warriors

Edge of Eon

Touch of Eon

Heart of Eon

Kiss of Eon

Mark of Eon

Claim of Eon

Storm of Eon

Soul of Eon

King of Eon

Also Available as Audiobooks!

Galactic Gladiators: House of Rone

Sentinel

Defender

Centurion

Paladin

Guard

Weapons Master

Also Available as Audiobooks!

Galactic Gladiators

Gladiator

Warrior

Hero

Protector

Champion

Barbarian

Beast

Rogue

Guardian

Cyborg

Imperator

Hunter

Also Available as Audiobooks!

Hell Squad

Marcus

Cruz

Gabe

Reed

Roth

Noah

Shaw

Holmes

Niko

Finn

Devlin

Theron

Hemi

Ash

Levi

Manu

Griff

Dom

Survivors

Tane

Also Available as Audiobooks!

The Anomaly Series

Time Thief

Mind Raider

Soul Stealer

Salvation

Anomaly Series Box Set

The Phoenix Adventures

Among Galactic Ruins

At Star's End

In the Devil's Nebula

On a Rogue Planet

Beneath a Trojan Moon

Beyond Galaxy's Edge

On a Cyborg Planet

Return to Dark Earth

On a Barbarian World

Lost in Barbarian Space

Through Uncharted Space

Crashed on an Ice World

Perma Series

Winter Fusion

A Galactic Holiday

Warriors of the Wind

Tempest

Storm & Seduction

Fury & Darkness

Standalone Titles

Savage Dragon

Hunter's Surrender

One Night with the Wolf

For more information visit www.annahackett.com

ABOUT THE AUTHOR

I'm a USA Today bestselling romance author who's passionate about ***fast-paced, emotion-filled*** contemporary romantic suspense and science fiction romance. I love writing about people overcoming unbeatable odds and achieving seemingly impossible goals. I like to believe it's possible for all of us to do the same.

I live in Australia with my own personal hero and two very busy, always-on-the-move sons.

For release dates, behind-the-scenes info, free books, and other fun stuff, sign up for the latest news here:

Website: www.annahackett.com

Made in United States
North Haven, CT
29 October 2023